Rewriting Fate

Patrick Townsend

Contents

Chapter 1

"Let's get divorced," Duke Henrick Audovera said, his voice cold and detached as he slid a neatly prepared set of documents across the desk.

Veronica froze, the words cutting through the air like a blade. For a moment, she stared at the papers, her vision blurring as tears welled up in her eyes.

"Divorce?" she repeated, her voice trembling as she looked up at him, searching his face for some sign of hesitation or remorse. There was none.

"How could you be so cruel?" Her voice broke, and the first tear slipped down her cheek, followed swiftly by another. "For three years, I waited for you. I prayed for your safe return every single day. I still loved you, even though you were away."

Her hands clenched the divorce papers, trembling with raw emotion.

"Divorce? Nonsense!" She ripped the papers in half with a sharp motion, the sound echoing in the silent office. The torn pages fluttered to the floor like fallen leaves.

"I will not sign those papers!" she declared, her voice fierce despite the tears streaking her face. Without another word, she turned on her heel and stormed out, slamming the door behind her.

Unbeknownst to her, that defiant act would mark the beginning of the end—the end of the doomed life Veronica had resigned herself to.

Duke Henrick Audovera was a name spoken with reverence throughout the Oriviel Empire. A pillar of strength and an unwavering shield, his prowess on the battlefield solidified the empire's borders and secured countless victories against neighboring kingdoms. His unmatched skills and unyielding loyalty made him a hero in the eyes of the people—and an object of fascination among the empire's young noblewomen.

Among his admirers was Lady Veronica Cosimo, the only daughter of Marquis Cosimo. Renowned for her ethereal beauty, Veronica was a fixture of high society, envied and admired in equal measure. Yet behind her flawless exterior lay a different truth: she was an arrogant and immature woman, accustomed to having the world at her feet and the wealth to indulge her every whim.

From the moment she set her sights on the young Duke, Veronica became obsessed. No other suitor could compare to him in her eyes, and she refused to entertain the idea of anyone else. Driven by her infatuation, she pressured her father relentlessly, until the Marquis—recognizing the benefits of such a match—used his influence to push the Duke into marriage.

Though Henrick harbored no affection for Veronica, he yielded to the Marquis' demands for reasons known only to himself. Thus, the Duke and the Marquis' daughter were wed in a grand ceremony, uniting two powerful families.

But their marriage was one of convenience, not love. Shortly after their union, the empire called upon its sword once more. A war broke out, demanding Henrick's presence on the battlefield.For three long years, the Duke fought at the empire's borders, his name resounding in every victory. During these years, far from the gilded halls of high society, he encountered someone unexpected, Irene Theano, a priestess of remarkable grace and unwavering conviction.

Irene's presence on the battlefield was as striking as it was unexpected. While Henrick commanded armies and cut through enemies with his blade, Irene offered solace and healing, her faith shining like a beacon in the chaos of war.

Henrick's love for Irene burned brighter than anything he had ever known, and with every passing day, his resolve to end his marriage with Veronica grew stronger. For him, their union was nothing more than an unwanted obligation—a barrier to the future he envisioned with the woman who had captured his heart.

But for Veronica, it was the opposite. Henrick was her world, the axis upon which her life spun. Her jealousy of Irene was not born of malice, but of a desperate yearning to hold onto the man she loved so deeply.

Her desperation, however, only led to her downfall. When Irene became the target of Veronica's envy, events spiraled out of control. A confrontation left Irene gravely injured, teetering on the brink of death. Henrick, furious and protective, came to her rescue and ensured her safety.

Veronica, left with no choice, finally conceded to the divorce. She signed the papers with trembling hands, her blackened heart splintering into pieces she could never mend.

The once-proud Duchess faded from society's gaze, her name whispered only in contempt. To the world, she was a villainess who deserved her fate, and her death was celebrated as the ultimate justice.

But the truth was far more painful. Veronica had never sought power or wealth—only the love of the man who had been her everything. She had played her role poorly, not out of cruelty, but out of the sheer impossibility of being the woman he wanted.

Thus ended the life of Veronica Audovera. Not with fireworks or grand retribution, but with the quiet, mournful extinguishing of a flame that had burned too brightly, too recklessly, and far too alone.

"Haaa... It would've been nice if I'd remembered all of this much earlier," I muttered, staring blankly at the ceiling of my lavish bedroom. Why did my memories have to come back now? Now that I'm already married to the male protagonist.

Yes, that male protagonist.

I wasn't always Veronica Cosimo—the Duchess of Audovera and soon-to-be villainess of this story. Once, I was just an ordinary teacher, living an ordinary life. Then one fateful evening, as I was crossing the street, a bus ended my uneventful existence.

And because the universe apparently has a twisted sense of humor, I was reborn as her.

It all clicked yesterday—a single day after my husband, Duke Henrick Audovera, left for war. My memories came flooding back, painting a clear picture of the disaster I'd unwittingly stepped into.

I had read this story before. I knew exactly how it end-ed. The Duchess of Audovera, villainess extraordinaire, would meet her demise after her husband divorced her and married Irene Theano, the saintly heroine.

And now, I'm Veronica.

I sighed deeply, dragging a hand down my face. Why couldn't I have been reborn as a random peasant in the countryside instead? No, I just had to be the villainess. And not just any villainess—the villainess. The one who caused property damage, tormented her servants, in-sulted nobles, and made a complete spectacle of her-self wherever she went. Oh, and let's not forget how I turned into a raging lunatic whenever anyone so much as glanced at Henrick.

It's no wonder I didn't have any friends.

Now, with my impending doom looming over me like a thundercloud, I've been scrambling to recall every detail of the novel. I need a plan—a foolproof strategy to save myself.

"Ah, whatever," I said with a dismissive wave of my hand, as if brushing off the weight of an entire storyline. "Let's just sign the divorce papers, get a massive alimony payout, and live peacefully in some faraway corner of the empire. Yeah, that's it. That's the plan. I'll be free in three years."

Who needs love, anyway? Certainly not me.

I grinned to myself, feeling a flicker of relief at my new-found resolve. "No more villainess nonsense. I'll just be the extra character who claps politely at their wedding. Yep, that's a solid plan."

For the first time since the memories resurfaced, I felt like I could breathe. I'd escape the chains of this storyline, leave the drama behind, and live a quiet, un-complicated life.

Or at least, that's what I told myself.

"Hahahahaha..." I laughed dryly, sprawled across the chaise in my room.

Three years. It's been three years, and I'm finally ready to sign those papers. In fact, I've practiced my signature repeatedly to ensure it's perfect. When the moment comes, I'll sign with elegance and grace—maybe even add a little flourish for dramatic effect.

He came home this morning. The Duke. My husband. Or rather, my soon-to-be ex-husband.I played the part of the dutiful Duchess, of course. When the grand gates opened to welcome his return, I was there, dressed to perfection, smiling like the happiest woman alive. I even greeted him warmly, though every word tasted bitter on my tongue.

"Welcome home, Your Grace," I'd said, curtseying with a smile so practiced it could fool even the most sea-soned of court ladies.

Inside, I was anything but pleased.

I'd read the novel. I knew how this scene played out. The Duke was supposed to summon me to his office immediately upon his return. There, he'd hand me the divorce papers, his voice detached and devoid of emotion.

I'd prepared for it. Braced myself for the blow.

So why, three days later, am I still waiting?

"Why hasn't he asked for a divorce?!" I groaned, pacing the length of my room like a caged animal.

This isn't how it's supposed to go! By now, I should've been halfway through planning my new, carefree life in a charming little countryside villa. Maybe sipping wine on a terrace while laughing at the memory of this wretched marriage.

Instead, I'm stuck here, drowning in confusion.

Could it be that he's waiting for the right moment? Or maybe he forgot? No, that's absurd—he's the Duke. He doesn't forget things.

I sank into a chair with a heavy sigh, my perfectly rehearsed plan unraveling before my eyes.

"Ugh, just get it over with already," I muttered under my breath, glaring at the door as if willing it to open.

The wait was unbearable. And worse, the uncertainty was starting to chip away at my resolve.

Chapter 2

It's been three fricking days. Why hasn't the Duke summoned me yet?

The longer I stay here, the more stressed I get. I'm completely ready for this divorce—what on earth is he waiting for?

"Duchess? A letter has arrived from Marquis Cosimo," Lucy, the head maid of the Audovera duchy, announced as she entered the room without knocking.

"From Father?" I said, raising an eyebrow. I took the letter and opened it immediately. "Thank you. You can leave now," I added with a small nod.

Since moving here, I've made it a rule not to let any maids linger in my room. I only call them when I need something, and even then, it's strictly business.

I don't know what it is, but I always have this nagging feeling that they're keeping an eye on me. Watching. Judging. And honestly? They probably are.

That's been the story of the past three years. It's not like anyone in this household acknowledges me as the Duchess anyway, but do I care? No, not one bit.

We're all just waiting, aren't we? Waiting for the day I pack up and leave.

With a resigned sigh, I unfolded the letter from Father.

To My Precious Daughter,

Today's weather is sunny and pleasant. I've heard the Duke has returned from the war. I hope you are doing well.

Two years ago, you requested a vacation house to be built within our territory. I'm pleased to inform you that the house is now complete. If there's anything you'd like to change, please let me know.

Whenever you wish to visit, I'll gladly accompany you.

Remember, my dear, this father of yours will always support you in whatever you plan.

Love,

Your Father

So, the house is finally done. Two years ago, I asked Father to build it for me. But truthfully, it was always meant to be my escape plan—a place to live after the divorce.

In this world, getting a divorce is like branding yourself with a scarlet letter. It's a stain on a woman's reputation, and I suppose that's why the original Veronica clung so desperately to her marriage. The shame of it all was just too much for her to bear.

But me? I couldn't care less. My reputation is already buried six feet under. I just want to live a quiet, peaceful life.

Setting the letter aside, I grabbed a sheet of paper and began writing my reply.

To My Dearest Father,

Thank you for delivering the wonderful news. I'm truly excited to see the vacation house. I'll let you know when it's a good time to visit.

I can't express how grateful I am for your unwavering support. Don't worry—your daughter is doing well here. I love and miss you. Please always take care of yourself.

With love,

Veronica

After sealing the letter, I called Lucy back to have it sent. Once she left my room, I let out a sigh of relief.

Well, that's one thing taken care of. I have a house waiting for me, complete with a swimming pool—my dream retreat. Now all that's left is the divorce and the alimony.

Cheers to my soon-to-be peaceful life!

I smiled to myself, imagining the house. When I first explained the concept of a swimming pool to Father, he was utterly baffled. I even attempted to draw it out, but my childish sketches didn't help much. Thankfully, the craftsman finally understood what I meant, and it all worked out.

"Now, what should I do?" I muttered, glancing around the massive room. One of the few perks of this marriage was living in such a grand house. The Duke and I hardly crossed paths, which was a blessing, especially now that he's back.

He's probably holed up in his office. Even after surviving a three-year war, he's drowning in paperwork. No rest for the mighty Duke, I suppose.

But me? I'm at my wit's end.

"I need to talk to someone. I need to vent, or I swear I'll lose my mind." I reached for the small bell on my desk and rang it, signaling for the servants.

At least one of them has to listen to me rant.

Lucy entered the room.

"Help me get dressed. I'm going to the palace," I said, and she immediately set to work.

The maids brought out a dress made from a smooth, delicate fabric, one that felt soft against the skin. There's a reason I always choose this type of clothing—it's comfortable and never irritates.Lucy and three other maids helped me prepare, and before long, I was ready.

"The carriage is ready, Duchess," Lucy informed me as she stood by the door.

By now, they were used to my occasional visits to the palace. However, Lucy paused before I could leave.

"You're not going to inform the Duke, Duchess?" she asked, causing me to stop in my tracks.

"S-should I?" I hesitated for a moment. Was that really necessary? "No, just tell him I visited a friend if he asks," I added with a shrug. Not that he'd bother asking—three days have passed since his return, and he hasn't even acknowledged me.

"To Baerth Castle," I told the coachman as I climbed into the carriage. It lurched forward, and I leaned back with a sigh.

Baerth Castle is where the Empress resides. She's the only person in this country I'd consider a friend, the only one I can talk to like a normal human being.

Here, in this lonely duchy, where even the servants keep their distance, her company is my sole reprieve.

Duke Henrick stood by the window, his sharp eyes fixed on the carriage rolling down the driveway.

"David, where is the Duchess going?" he asked, his voice calm but laced with curiosity, never once glancing at the head butler standing behind him.

"The Duchess is heading to Baerth Castle, Your Grace," David replied dutifully.

"Baerth Castle? The Empress's palace?" Evander, the Duke's aide and trusted knight, chimed in with a raised eyebrow.

"Yes, sir," David confirmed. "The Duchess often visits the Empress from time to time."

Evander crossed his arms, a skeptical look on his face. "Hmm. Were they always that close? What is she scheming this time?"

The Duke, unfazed by the speculation, turned back to his desk, his expression unreadable. Instead of indulging in Evander's musings, he redirected the conversation.

"Did you retrieve the things I requested?" he asked David, his tone flat but authoritative.

"Yes, Your Grace. These are the ledgers documenting all of the Duchess's expenditures over the past three years." David stepped forward, carefully placing the thick stack of ledgers on the desk.

Henrick opened the first book, flipping through the pages with deliberate precision. Veronica's reputation as a spendthrift preceded her, and he fully expected to see extravagant numbers—jewelry, dresses, feasts. Yet, he was unprepared for what he saw.

"Is this accurate?" the Duke asked, his brow furrowing as disbelief flickered across his usually stoic face.

"Yes, Your Grace," David affirmed. "I personally veri-fied each entry."

"What is it?" Evander asked, leaning closer to take a peek at the pages.

"Impossible," Henrick muttered, still staring at the numbers in front of him.

Evander scanned the records, his own expression twisting in confusion. "What... what did she even do with all this money? It's nowhere near what we expected."

The Duke closed the ledger with a soft but firm thud, his mind reeling. "What has she been doing all these years?" he murmured, more to himself than anyone else.

Something didn't add up. The woman he remembered from before the war—the one who demanded luxury and attention at every turn—was not reflected in these records.

And for the first time in years, Henrick found himself deeply curious about the woman he'd married.

Chapter 3

"Judging by that expression on your face, things didn't quite go as planned, did they?" came the sudden arrival of Empress Adelaide Schumann Oriviel.

"I greet Your Imperial Majesty, Empress Adelaide," I said, standing to greet her.We were currently seated in the drawing room of Baerth Castle, a place that always felt a little too grand for my tastes.

"Have a seat, Duchess Veronica," she said, gesturing gracefully as the servants brought out tea and an assortment of delicacies. Once everything was arranged, the Empress subtly waved the servants away, granting us privacy.

"So, tell me, Veronica. What happened? You're wearing such a grim expression. Did the Duke already divorce you?" she asked, her piercing gaze locking onto mine as she leaned forward, clearly invested in my plight.

"That's just it! He hasn't!" I threw my hands up in exasperation. "What's wrong with him? Did he hit his head during the war or something?"

At that, Empress Adelaide burst into laughter, her melodious voice filling the room. "Oh, Veronica, you never fail to amuse me. Tell me more. I need to know every detail of this saga."

I sighed, slumping slightly in my chair. "What's there to tell? It's been three days since he returned, and I was ready—absolutely ready—to sign those papers. I even practiced my signature for it! But instead of asking for a divorce, he's been holed up in his office. No acknowledgment, no confrontation, nothing!"

The Empress shook her head, her amusement still evident. "Perhaps he's testing you. Or maybe..." She paused, her eyes gleaming with mischief. "He has other plans in mind."

I groaned, burying my face in my hands. "Please, don't even joke about that. All I want is to be free of this ridiculous marriage and live my life in peace. Is that too much to ask?"

Adelaide took a sip of her tea, a knowing smile playing on her lips. "Oh, Veronica, nothing is ever simple when it comes to men like Henrick. I have a feeling this is just the beginning of your little adventure."

I couldn't decide whether to laugh or cry. Somehow, this was turning out to be far more complicated than I'd anticipated.

"Maybe the Duke doesn't want to divorce you," Empress Adelaide said with a sly smile. "Why are you so adamant about getting a divorce, anyway? Isn't the Duke your first love or something?"

The question hit harder than it should have, but there was no way I could tell her the real reason—the one ripped straight from the novel's plot. She'd probably think I'd lost my mind.

"It's just a one-sided love," I said with a shrug, keeping my tone as casual as possible. "I want to get a divorce because I feel bad about it. Because of my immaturity, he was forced to marry me. Besides, aren't we practically strangers? I think it's better to end it sooner rather than later."

And it's true—this marriage has no future. If you can even call it a marriage.

The war broke out not long after our wedding, and Henrick left almost immediately. Before the wedding, we barely even spoke to each other. Most of our "interactions" consisted of me stalking him from afar, only to swoop in and confront any woman who dared to approach him.

Thinking back, I wouldn't blame him if he thought I was insane—everyone else certainly did.The Empress regarded me with a thoughtful expression before offering a small sigh. "Well, since you're so serious about it, then, as your friend, I'll support you."

Her words were sincere, but the teasing glint in her eye made me wonder just how much she believed me.

"Thanks," I said with a weak smile. "I'll need all the support I can get."

Adelaide leaned back in her chair, swirling her teacup. "But you know, Veronica, it's rather interesting. For someone so determined to leave, you still seem... affected by him."

I froze for a moment, her words catching me off guard. Was it that obvious? I shook my head, dismissing the thought. No, this wasn't about feelings anymore—it was about survival. And freedom.

"Well, whatever the reason, you're always welcome here," Adelaide said, offering a warm smile."Thanks," I repeated, more earnestly this time. At least I had one ally in this mess.

Looking back, I never thought I'd end up being friends with the Empress of this country. Honestly, no one else expected it either. We're complete opposites. Empress Adelaide is the epitome of kindness and grace, while I...

well, let's just say I'm not winning any sainthood awards anytime soon.

Before becoming the Empress, she was already the star of high society. As the daughter of Duke Schumann, she was practically destined for the role of Empress. There was no competition—she was the perfect candidate in every way.

As we chatted, I found myself rambling on about all the trivial things I had done during those stressful three days. Most of it was nonsense, really, but Adelaide laughed at nearly everything I said. I wasn't trying to be funny, yet there she was, laughing so much she started coughing.

"Are you okay, Your Imperial Majesty?" I asked, genuinely concerned as she struggled to catch her breath.

"Yes, I'm okay," she assured me between coughs, waving her hand. "My apologies for worrying you."

I frowned, unconvinced. "I think I should leave now so you can rest. I'll visit you again next time.""Time does fly when you're enjoying yourself," Adelaide said with a warm smile. "Then, I'll see you again soon, Duchess."

With that, I stood and began making my way out of Baerth Castle. As I stepped into the carriage, I couldn't help but marvel at how my unlikely friendship with the Empress had become a bright spot in this chaotic life.

Empress Adelaide had been in poor health ever since giving birth to the princess two years ago. It's been two years now since we became friends, and in that time, I've come to realize just how fragile she is. When I first started visiting her, it was because I needed her help—before and after we became friends. But over time, something changed.

I knew from the novel that she would die, though her death was only briefly mentioned. Her body, worn out from years of stress, would eventually give in. That knowledge weighs on me heavily, especially since I can see how much she's struggling now.

That's why I visit her so often. I don't do it out of pity for her impending death or because she helped me when I needed it. I do it because she accepted me, flaws and all. She saw beyond the villainess role I was cast in and offered her friendship without hesitation. I genuinely like her, and I don't want her to be alone in her remaining days.

Her kindness means more to me than she'll ever know. It's a rare thing to find someone who accepts you as you are, especially when you've been condemned as a villain. Yet she did just that, and I'll always be grateful to her for it.

After my visit to Baerth Castle, I headed home. As soon as I got out of the carriage, I was surprised to see David, Duke Henrick's butler, waiting for me.

"Welcome home, Duchess. You are being summoned by the Duke," he said, a smile on his face. Oh my god, is this it?

"Oh, okay. Then I'll meet the Duke now," I said quickly, walking inside. As I made my way to his office, David stopped me.

"The Duke is in the drawing room," he said, which only confused me more.

"Huh? The drawing room? Why is he calling me there?" I asked. Instead of answering, David just smiled and opened the door for me.

"Your Grace, the Duchess is here," he announced.

My smile immediately disappeared as I entered the drawing room. I had expected to find Duke Henrick and maybe his lawyer for the divorce papers, but instead, there were several gowns on display. What the heck is this?

"I happily greet the Duchess of Audovera," a woman greeted me.

"Madam Luisa? What are you doing here?" I asked her. Madam Luisa was a designer and the owner of Atkins Atelier, the place where the trendiest and most expensive dresses were made. I knew that because I had once been one of their VIP customers.

"What are you talking about, Duchess? The Duke booked us for your gown for the upcoming banquet," she replied, further confusing me.

"Banquet?" I asked, my eyes immediately shifting to Duke Henrick, who was sitting quietly, watching us. When our eyes met, I quickly looked away.

What banquet was this? "Follow me, Duchess," Madam Luisa said, pulling me toward the fitting room. "Since it's been a while since you visited the atelier, I'll need to take your new measurements," she added, pulling out a tape measure and beginning to take my measurements.

"But Madam Luisa, what is this banquet you're talking about?" I asked, completely distracted. What about the divorce?

"Oh my goodness, Duchess. Sometimes you ask strange questions. There will be a banquet at the palace to celebrate the victory of the recent war," she explained.

"Oh, that banquet," I said, finally understanding. I remembered it from the novel. "I'm invited?" I asked, bewildered. From what I remembered, I wasn't invited, and after the divorce, I would be too embarrassed to attend.

"Of course, you are invited," Madam Luisa replied, almost as if saying "duh." I fell silent, noticing that she was starting to get weirded out by my questions and actions.

After Madam Luisa finished measuring me, I thought I was done, but no—there were still a ton of gowns to try on. What made it worse was that I had to show Duke Henrick the ones I tried on.

Why was he choosing my outfits?! What the hell was happening?!

Chapter 4

I lost count of how many dresses I had tried on. I was exhausted, feeling like all my energy had been drained. What annoyed me even more was that with each dress I tried on, the Duke always had something to say about it.

Seriously, what the heck is going on? Why is he suddenly my fashion stylist? Did he hit his head or something? If I have to try on one more dress, I might lose it.

"That's the last one, Your Grace," Madam Luisa said, which made me incredibly relieved. Finally! I rushed back to the fitting room to change, but my frustration grew when I heard Duke Henrick's next words to Madam Luisa.

"I'm going to buy everything she tried on."

I swear my ears practically burned at that moment. Why did I even bother trying everything on if you're just going to buy them all anyway?

Why are you doing this to me? Am I being punished for something? Is this my punishment for forcing you to marry me?

After I finished changing, I quickly left the fitting room, intending to talk to the Duke about the banquet, but instead, I was sent straight to my room. I grabbed the back of my neck, trying to calm myself. My blood pressure was through the roof.

Due to sheer exhaustion, I fell asleep as soon as I lay down on my bed. Honestly, though, what is wrong with the Duke? He's acting so strange lately.

Meanwhile, after sending Veronica to her room, Duke Henrick resumed his work, heading to his office. Ever since their return from the war, there's been a noticeable shift in how he's been treating the Duchess. On the other hand, Evander Nesta, his trusted aide, kept casting suspicious glances at him.

Evander has never been fond of Veronica. His hostility toward her was apparent even before their marriage. People have been saying that the Duchess has changed, but Evander isn't convinced. He believes that she's still up to something, waiting for the right moment to strike.

Several days passed, and Veronica couldn't shake the restlessness. She waited for Duke Henrick to summon her, but it never happened. She even tried going to him, but either he wasn't around or he was too busy with other matters. The tension built with every passing day, and just as she was starting to lose hope, the day of the banquet finally arrived.

I am currently being prepared by the maids for the banquet tonight. My dress had a stunning combination of royal blue and silver, and the style was undeniably elegant. However, the slit in the dress was so high that I had to accessorize my legs as well. The preparations started around noon, and even as the sun began to set, we weren't done yet.

Honestly, I am nervous. I know what is going to happen at the banquet, at least from Irene's perspective, the female protagonist. But as for Veronica? I have no idea what awaits me. I still have plenty of enemies there. Ugh!

After several hours, one of the maids entered to inform me that Duke Henrick was calling for me. Why didn't he come himself? They made me wear these killer silver heels. Killer because they were so high. It's been a while since I wore shoes like this, and I am sure I'll get blisters.

After a few retouches, I started walking. I didn't want to keep the Duke waiting any longer, and certainly not Evander, who I knew hated me. Psh!

When I reached the stairs, I saw Duke Henrick standing at the bottom. Ugh! He really is handsome!

I quickly looked away when our eyes met. If this had happened before, I would've been thrilled, overjoyed that he was looking at me like that. But now... I don't know. I cautiously descended the stairs, aware that I could fall at any moment. Why did they give me such tall shoes? And with this slit in the dress, it was a disaster waiting to happen. It was way too revealing—I'm pretty sure my underwear was showing.

Halfway down, it seemed like Duke Henrick finally realized and came to help me. Out of the corner of my eye, I saw Evander's frown.

Hmph! I don't care about you!

Now that it was just the two of us inside the carriage, my anxiety doubled. This is so crazy. I wore my usual poker face and stared out the window, but deep inside, I was panicking. The silence felt so awkward, and... why the hell is he staring at me like that?! It only made me more self-conscious.

I swear, I could feel the sweat building up under my armpits. The entire ride, I did my best to avoid the Duke's intense gaze. Goodness, we hadn't even reached the venue yet, and I already felt like 50% of my energy had been drained.

While Veronica did her best to avoid the Duke's intense gaze, Duke Henrick, on the other hand, was deep in thought about her. Compared to the Veronica he had known three years ago—the one who had clung to him obsessively—the woman sitting across from him now was strikingly different. Gone was the desperate longing in her eyes; instead, he could sense that she was intentionally avoiding him.

The change was subtle, but it was there. Her posture, her gaze—everything about her spoke of distance, as if she had put up a wall that was keeping him out. He couldn't help but wonder: what had happened to her? Why had she changed so much? It troubled him, but at the same time, he couldn't quite put his finger on why it bothered him so much.

After that long and exhausting ride, we finally arrived at the palace. My surprise doubled when Duke Henrick suddenly offered his hand to help me out of the carriage. Oh right, we're married. We need to put on a show, pretending everything is fine between us—even when it isn't. Without much thought, I accepted his hand, reminding myself it was all part of the act.

Walking into the grand banquet hall felt strange. It had been three years since I last attended such a gathering. The opulence of the place hadn't changed, but the weight of all those eyes on us certainly added to my discomfort.

"Entering the hall, His Grace, Duke Henrick Audovera, and Her Grace, Duchess Veronica Audovera," the announcer bellowed, his voice echoing through the room. Could he be any louder? I tried not to roll my eyes.

As expected, the moment we stepped inside, all attention turned toward us. Or rather, toward Duke Henrick. It wasn't a surprise. With his striking features and commanding presence, paired with the fact that tonight's celebration was in his honor, he was the undeniable center of attraction.

Within moments, we were swarmed. People approached us with flattering smiles and endless greetings, most of which were directed at him. Compliments flew left and right, all with undertones of opportunistic sincerity. It was exhausting.

Sensing there was no point in lingering, I slipped away at the first opportunity. "Excuse me," I murmured with a practiced smile before distancing myself from the Duke and his admirers.

Grabbing a glass of champagne from a passing waiter, I found a quiet corner with fewer people—a sanctuary where I could observe the spectacle of pretense without participating in it. After all, social gatherings like this were a game of masks, and I wasn't in the mood to play.

It's a shame the empress couldn't attend tonight. She would've made this evening bearable. I heard her cough had worsened, which only added to my worries. I wished there was something I could do for her. Even in the novel, her illness remained a mystery. With no answers from the story and no modern medical knowledge at my disposal, I felt helpless.

Lost in thought, I barely noticed the growing commotion near the entrance. The crowd seemed to buzz with increasing excitement. What is it this time? These people are like moths to a flame—always flocking to drama.

Curiosity tugged at me, but I stayed rooted in my corner, quietly sipping my champagne.

"Entering the hall, Priestess Irene Theano," the announcer's voice rang loud and clear.My head instinctively turned toward the entrance, and there she was—the female protagonist herself, Irene Theano.

Dressed in an immaculate white gown that flowed like liquid starlight, she seemed to radiate an otherworldly aura. Her hair cascaded down her back like a shimmering waterfall, and the faintest trace of a serene smile graced her face as she entered.

There was no doubt about it. Irene Theano was the epitome of grace and beauty. It was as if she had stepped out of the pages of a fairytale. The crowd parted before her, their collective gazes filled with awe and reverence.

It made sense. In this world, Irene wasn't just a noblewoman or a beauty. She was the Priestess, a figure of divine significance, said to have been chosen by the gods themselves. She wasn't just admired—she was revered.

And here I was, standing in the corner with a champagne glass in hand, feeling like a mere backdrop to her radiance. The heroine had made her grand entrance, and the story was already shifting around her.

Chapter 5

Whoa. That's Irene Theano?

I instinctively covered my mouth, trying to stifle my surprise. No wonder Duke Henrick fell for her. She's stunning—like she just stepped out of a painting—and the white dress complements her perfectly. I wasn't the only one captivated; everyone else at the banquet had the same reaction.

Moments later, Emperor Darius Franz Czar Oriviel began his congratulatory speech, commending those who had returned victorious from the war. All eyes were on him, attentively listening to every word. Well, all eyes except mine. I couldn't help but roll them.

Ugh, the emperor. Just the sight of him is enough to sour my mood.

As soon as his overly long speech ended, the music began, signaling the start of the evening's dances. Not my thing. I'd rather stay here and keep a low profile.

But my attention was drawn to the center of the dance hall. There they were—Duke Henrick and Irene, standing together.

Whoa. Amazing. This is straight out of the novel.

I won't deny it—they look perfect together. Even the people around them couldn't stop murmuring their admiration. Compliments poured in like a steady stream of whispers: "What a handsome couple," "So regal," "They're a match made in heaven."

Unfortunately, some of those whispers were also directed at me. A few people sneaked glances in my direction, curious about how the "villainess" would react.

Ah, the perks of being a public spectacle. Lovely.

Normally, I would've caused a scene, unleashing my fury on any woman who dared get close to Duke Henrick. But today? Nah. I flashed a sweet, polite smile at those waiting for my meltdown. Their confused expressions were priceless. Sorry to disappoint, folks, but I couldn't care less about what's happening.

Honestly, I wanted to leave. My eyes wandered back to the Duke and Priestess Irene, standing under the soft glow of the chandeliers. People around them were teasing them to dance, just like in the novel.

And then, they did.

Their dance was elegant and undeniably romantic, like something straight out of a fairytale. For a brief moment, I felt like I was watching a romantic movie. I even found myself smiling unconsciously.

But the smile quickly faded when a strange pang hit me.

Ugh. We really should finalize that divorce.

I turned away, pretending to sip my champagne, but when I glanced back, our eyes locked. Duke Henrick was looking straight at me.

My heart nearly leaped out of my chest.

Seriously? Out of all these people here, you still managed to spot me?

To save myself from further awkwardness, I hurriedly left the banquet hall, escaping into the crisp night air. The cold breeze hit me like a sudden splash of water, and I instinctively hugged myself. Right. I forgot how revealing this dress was.

Not wanting to go back inside and face that suffocating crowd, I wandered into the garden instead. It was quiet, serene—exactly what I needed to gather myself. Ever since we arrived, I'd been feeling weird, like there was something heavy pressing down on me.

Better to deal with this out here than in there, surrounded by prying eyes.

I checked my surroundings to ensure I was alone. The darkness and sparse lighting were perfect. Satisfied, I exhaled deeply and rested a hand on my stomach.

And then it happened.

Oh, no.

I knew it. I knew my fart would make a sound!

I slapped my hands over my mouth, my face burning with embarrassment—even though there was no one around. I'd been holding it in since the carriage ride, but with Duke Henrick sitting right next to me, there was no way I could let it out. My stomach had been cramping all night because of it!

Finally, sweet, gassy relief.

"Pfft--"

I spun around, startled by the stifled laughter. When I saw who it was, I wanted the ground to open up and swallow me whole.

"Y-Your Majesty?" I blurted, barely able to contain my embarrassment. What in the world was the emperor doing here?

"Duchess Veronica," Emperor Darius Franz Czar Oriviel said between barely contained chuckles. "Pfft—ha! I was wondering why you were out here all alone. Haha—I didn't mean to, but pffttt—" He broke into a full laugh, and my annoyance spiked. This is exactly why I can't stand this man!

Let me paint you a picture: Emperor Darius, ruler of this vast country, a man eight years my senior, is currently acting like a child who just heard a fart joke for the first time. How he became emperor remains one of life's greatest mysteries. Were there no other candidates?

"Hahaha!" His laughter continued unabated, his broad shoulders shaking with amusement. "There's never a dull day with you, Duchess Veronica," he managed to say, and I scowled in response. What nonsense was going to come out of his mouth next?

"Your Majesty, if you've had your fill of laughing at me, I'll take my leave," I said, barely masking my irritation.

Still chuckling, he waved a hand dismissively. "Relax, Duchess. Kidding aside, I wanted to update you about Adelaide's condition."

At the mention of the Empress, his expression shifted. The mirth drained from his face, replaced by a somber seriousness that caught me off guard. "I truly appreciate everything you've done for Adelaide and our daughter, Alicia," he said quietly. "But her condition has worsened. As you know, I've hired the best physicians, the most skilled healers I could find, and yet none of them have been able to identify her illness or its cause. Useless fools." His frustration was palpable, his words edged with bitterness.

I stared at him, my own irritation forgotten. The Emperor, usually so flippant and carefree, now seemed burdened by a weight too heavy for even a ruler to bear.

The Empress's illness feels like an unsolvable riddle, a puzzle with missing pieces. Even in the novel, it was left shrouded in mystery. I genuinely want to help her, but without more information, I feel helpless. I'd even suggested hiring the genius doctors I'd read about in the novel, but their conclusions were all the same.

There's no cure.

"Thank you for telling me, Your Majesty," I said softly, the weight of his words settling over me. He was indirectly preparing me for what was inevitable—the Empress's passing. Despite knowing this from the novel, facing the reality of it still made my heart ache.

"I know your relationship with Adelaide is precious to you," the Emperor continued, his expression heavy with sincerity. "And I'm certain she treasures it just as much. I only hope that, when the time comes, I can still rely on your assistance, Duchess Veronica."

His words made me frown. Assistance?

"Pardon, Your Majesty?" I asked, my confusion clear. What kind of assistance was he talking about? But before I could press him for clarification, a sudden force pulled me away.

I staggered slightly before glancing up. "D-Duke?" I stammered, my eyes wide. It was Henrick, his grip firm on my wrist. His sudden appearance and actions left me utterly baffled. What on earth was he doing here?

I staggered slightly before glancing up. "D-Duke?" I stammered, my eyes wide. It was Henrick, his grip firm on my wrist. His sudden appearance and actions left me utterly baffled. What on earth was he doing here?

Chapter 6

"Duke?" My voice wavered as I stared at him, utterly confused. Why is he here? What about the party inside? What about the dance? And... why are his hands on my waist?

"Hmm? This is quite a shock. I don't think I've ever seen you react like this before, Duke Henrick." Emperor Darius's amused voice cut through my thoughts. "Don't worry, Duchess Veronica and I were merely catching up. I'll leave you two to... whatever this is." He gave me a playful smirk before sauntering away, leaving me alone with Henrick.

What the hell was that?

We both watched as the emperor walked off, neither saying a word until he disappeared from view. Only then did I realize Henrick's hand was still firmly on my waist. My body stiffened before I abruptly stepped back, creating some much-needed space.

"W-What are you doing here, Your Grace?" I asked, trying to keep my voice steady.

"Why did you leave?" he countered, completely ignoring my question and throwing one of his own.

"I— I needed some air," I replied, though the words felt flimsy. Okay, technically true... but I'm not about to tell him the real reason. Not in a million years.

His eyes narrowed slightly. "What were you and the emperor talking about?"

"The emperor was simply informing me about the Empress's current condition," I said truthfully.

"And since when did the two of you get so close?" His tone sharpened, his expression unreadable.

"Pardon?" I blinked, utterly taken aback. What is this? A surprise Q&A session?

"Me and the emperor? Ew— I mean," I corrected myself hastily, "I am not in any kind of close relationship with the emperor. Far from it, Your Grace."

His gaze lingered on me for a moment longer, as though he was trying to decide whether or not to believe me.

The Duke continued to scrutinize me, his eyes sharp and calculating, as if trying to determine if I was lying. Am I really going to lie now? I asked myself. There's nothing to gain from lying, especially when we're talking about the emperor—the ruler of this entire country.

I'm not ambitious enough to want anything from that good-for-nothing. Honestly, I think he just sees me as a joke. Every time he looks at me, he laughs, even when nothing is funny.

Suddenly, a gust of wind blew through the air, and I instinctively wrapped my arms around myself.

"Ah... Duke, you don't have to," I protested, seeing him begin to remove his coat.

"You might catch a cold, Veronica," he said, and before I could stop him, he draped the coat over my shoulders.

"T-thank you, Your Grace," I stammered, my voice faltering. I don't even need the coat, but why is it so hard to speak right now? The warmth of the coat only seemed to make my face heat up, especially when he said my name. This was the first time he had called me by my name, and I couldn't stop the flush that spread across my cheeks.

I quickly turned my face away, hoping he wouldn't notice.

Slap!

In an attempt to shake myself out of my thoughts, I slapped my own face. Duke Henrick looked at me in surprise. "Why did you slap yourself?"

"Ah, it's n-nothing," I muttered, trying to laugh it off. Just needed to snap myself out of it.

No more lingering feelings. You've moved on. You don't have feelings for this man anymore, Veronica.

I repeated those words in my head, over and over. This mantra had been my lifeline for the past three years.

So what if he called my name? It's not a big deal. And for the second time, the Duke gave me a weird look. I know, it might seem strange, but I'm actually normal.

"Let's head back inside," he said, his voice calm.

"Actually, Your Grace..." I raised my right hand to speak, but then immediately lowered it as I realized what I was doing. Is this some kind of recitation?

"What is it?" he asked, furrowing his brow.

"I was going to ask if I could go home now since I'm not feeling well," I replied. It's probably fine for me to leave early. This party isn't really for me anyway. Whether I'm here or not doesn't matter.

The Duke paused for a moment, as if thinking about it. What's there to think about? "Fine," he agreed, and I couldn't help but feel a sense of victory. Yes! I'm finally going home.

"Aah!" Suddenly, the Duke scooped me up into his arms. "What are you doing? Wait, Your Grace?" I said, my heart racing as he began walking without hesitation.

"We're going home, just like you said," he replied, but I quickly realized I was the only one going home.

"But—" Wait! Why are you going back into the banquet hall? "Your Grace, could you please put me down?" I asked, feeling panic rise as we entered the hall, and all eyes turned to us.

I just know they'll think I'm making a scene, trying to draw attention. More importantly, this is so embarrassing. "Your Grace?" I pleaded again. "Please, put me down."

"Stay still. You're not feeling well," he said, as though his previous words were an excuse. All I could do was bury my face in my hands, hoping no one would notice how red it was from the humiliation.

What's wrong with you? Why are you like this?!

He carried me all the way to the carriage. I had planned to go back on my own, but what happened? I could only scratch my head and turn my eyes to the window. But to be honest, I had no more energy left. I leaned my head against the side of the carriage and closed my eyes. This is going to be a long ride again.

"... Congratulations on winning the war, Your Grace. Blah...blah...blah," Duke Henrick, already growing irritated as people continued to approach him.

Nosy people, he thought, his patience thinning. He ignored the conversations around him and scanned the crowd, searching for the Duchess. After a moment, he spotted her in a corner, sitting alone. He started moving toward her, but as he took a step, some of the war participants greeted him.

It wasn't until the priestess from the church arrived that he was finally unable to reach the Duchess.

"Good evening, Your Grace, The Duke of Audovera," Irene greeted him, her voice sweet and serene.

"Good evening, Priestess," he replied, keeping the exchange short and casual. It wasn't anything special, but to the onlookers, it seemed significant.

As the music started, people began whispering, their expectations rising. They wanted to see the Duke and the Priestess dance. Though reluctant, the Duke asked Irene for a dance, reasoning that it was just part of his duties as a war hero.

While they danced, the Duke's eyes drifted to the Duchess, who was watching them from the corner. He was a bit surprised to see her smiling, though it seemed like a distant, almost melancholic smile compared to her usual sharp reactions. Their eyes met for a moment, and the Duke noticed a subtle shift in her expression—a mixture of emotions he couldn't quite read—before she turned and left the banquet hall.

It left him feeling unsettled.

"Follow her, Your Grace," Irene's voice broke through the Duke's thoughts. He turned to her, confused, and she repeated, "Follow the Duchess, Your Grace."

Without hesitating, Duke Henrick immediately turned and headed for the door, intent on finding Veronica. His steps were quick, his mind preoccupied.

It took him longer than he expected to find her, weaving through the crowds, but when he finally spotted her, he was surprised by the sight that greeted him. Veronica wasn't alone—she was with the emperor. A knot twisted in his stomach at the sight of the two of them together, an uncomfortable feeling creeping over him.

His instincts kicked in, and without thinking, he approached them. The moment he was close enough, he reached out, pulling Veronica away from the emperor with an authoritative grip.

As he did, a surge of something unfamiliar washed over him. He could feel the change within himself. Something had shifted. The Duke couldn't explain it, but the sight of Veronica with the emperor stirred something in him—a realization, or perhaps a change he couldn't yet fully comprehend.

Duke Henrick noticed that Veronica had fallen asleep during the ride in the carriage. Without making a sound, he shifted closer and gently leaned her head onto his shoulder. As he watched her sleep, a soft expression crossed his face. There was something about her peaceful slumber that made her seem even more beautiful than usual.

The carriage finally arrived at the Audovera estate, but the Duke didn't have the heart to wake her. She was sleeping so soundly, so he decided to carry her. With careful steps, he lifted Veronica from the carriage and carried her inside, not wanting to disturb her rest.

The servants stared at them in shock, their eyes wide with surprise. Even Evander stood frozen, gaping at the scene before him. The Duke paid no attention to their gazes as he carefully walked through the estate and into her room. He gently lowered Veronica onto her bed, making sure she was comfortable, then tucked her in with a soft blanket.

As he stood beside her, watching her sleep, the Duke couldn't help but whisper, "Good night, Veronica." With the lightest of touches, he kissed her forehead, a tender gesture that spoke of emotions he hadn't yet fully realized.

The next morning, I woke up in my room, confused. I was just in the carriage, so how did I end up here? Tsk. I don't want to think about what happened last night. It'll only stress me out.

knock-knock

"Are you awake, Duchess?" Lucy's voice came from outside my room.

"Yes, come in," I replied, and Lucy, my maid, entered, holding a basin of warm water for me.

"Good morning, Duchess. I've brought warm water," she said, setting the basin down for me to wash up. I got up and started my usual morning routine. Hmm? At least there's something for my skincare here.

After getting ready and having breakfast, I decided to take a walk outside. I chose to walk far from my room, the office, or anywhere the Duke might be.

I need to come up with a plan. I've been here for too long. Everything is set up for my divorce, except the divorce itself. Plus, I should have a letter from my father by now. I think I'll check with the butler.

As I was deep in thought, I realized I had wandered into the training grounds. That's why I could hear the clanking of swords. I should head back now. The knights are still annoyed with me. They'll probably get annoyed if they see me.

I quickly turned to leave, but just as I did, they came out. Terrible timing! Looks like they were finishing up their training. I was even more surprised when they greeted me.

"Greetings, Duchess of Audovera," they all bowed. This is so awkward. I noticed how tired they looked from the sweat dripping down their faces.

"You may rise. You've been working hard even after the war," I said, though I wondered if they had any plans to rest or take a break. They should have at least a small celebration. They were the ones who went to war and risked their lives. The nobles who only participated in the banquet had nothing to do with the war. Ugh! Now that I'm thinking about it, the banquet lost its real purpose.

"Lucy?" I called for my maid.

"Yes, Duchess?"

"Tell the head maid in the kitchen to prepare refreshments for the knights... immediately," I said, and that should be enough. I just wanted to get out of here.

"Right away, Duchess," she nodded. I was about to leave when I heard the knights thanking me. Anyway, I need to get out of here.

"Thank you, Duchess."

"As expected of the Angel of War..."

I furrowed my brows at that, but I kept walking until I was far enough away. What the heck is the Angel of War?

"Your Grace, here are the letters that need your immediate attention," Butler David said as he handed a stack of letters to Duke Henrick, who immediately accepted them.

The Duke's eyes fell on one particular letter still in the butler's hand. "What about that letter?"

"Ah! This is a letter from Marquis Cosimo addressed to the Duchess," David explained, momentarily pausing in his task.

"The Duchess and her father have been exchanging letters frequently for the past three years," Butler David added.

"Oh? What are they scheming now?" Evander asked, leaning forward.

"Read the letter, David," Duke Henrick ordered.

"Are you sure, Your Grace? You might be invading the Duchess's privacy. She may be upset about it," David hesitated.

"Don't make me repeat myself, David. Read the contents of the letter," Duke Henrick commanded firmly.

Reluctantly, the butler opened the letter and read it in silence. For the past three years, he'd been keeping a close watch on the Duchess, already having some suspicions about her intentions. But as he read the letter from Cosimo, his suspicions were confirmed.

"What is it, David?" Evander asked, noticing the butler's change in expression.

"It seems the Duchess is preparing for a divorce."

Chapter 7

Duke Henrick dropped the papers he was holding, stunned by Butler David's revelation. "Divorce?" he repeated, his voice barely a whisper.

"Your Grace?" Evander, who had also been taken aback by the news, watched as Duke Henrick suddenly stood up and snatched the letter from David's hand. As he read about the house prepared for Veronica, as mentioned by Marquis Cosimo, his face darkened. Without warning, he began tearing the letter into pieces. "So she was planning on leaving me? Forcing me to marry her first, then leave me? Unforgivable."

"Summon the Duchess!" he ordered sharply.

"Right away, Your Grace," Butler David responded quickly, rushing out of the Duke's office. Evander stood silently at the side, acutely aware of Duke Henrick's visible fury.

Moments later, Butler David returned, his anxiety evident. "Where is she?" Duke Henrick demanded.

"It appears the Duchess has gone to Baerth Castle, Your Grace," Butler David replied, wincing as he awaited the Duke's reaction.

Duke Henrick closed his eyes briefly, clearly frustrated. "Go get my horse, Evander," he commanded.

Evander opened his mouth to respond but hesitated when he met the Duke's fierce glare."I understand, Your Grace," he said, nodding quickly.

Without another word, the Duke abandoned his work and set out to find Veronica, determined to confront her at Baerth Castle.

Duke Henrick spurred his horse into a gallop, pushing it faster than usual. In no time, he arrived at the palace, causing quite a stir. It was well-known that the Duke rarely visited the palace unless summoned by the Emperor. But today, he didn't bother with the Emperor's residence and went straight to Baerth Castle, where Veronica had gone.

Upon arriving at the castle, he dismounted quickly, handing his horse to the guards. Normally, what the Duke was doing would be considered rude, but no one dared to challenge the war hero. His aura alone, thick with tension and unspoken command, warned everyone to stay out of his way. The servants in Baerth Castle, uncertain of what was happening, reluctantly escorted him inside.

As he moved through the halls, to his surprise, he encountered the Emperor. "Quite a surprise to see you here, Henrick," the Emperor commented, his tone light. Duke Henrick only shot him a cold glance in response.

"Are you here to see the Empress?" the Emperor continued, but before Henrick could respond, the Emperor smirked. "Is what I want to ask, but obviously, you are here for the Duchess," he said, pointing toward Veronica, who was playing with Princess Alicia in the distance. "She's over there."

Duke Henrick's eyes darkened further. Every muscle in his body tensed as he looked at Veronica, feeling a mix of confusion, anger, and hurt. His mind raced with thoughts of what she might be planning, the divorce, the letter, and now, seeing her so carefree and innocent with the Princess.

After walking outside, I decided to visit Empress Adelaide since the Emperor had mentioned her condition had worsened. There wasn't much for me to do here, so I figured it would be better to go there.

I had Lucy help me change clothes and asked her to prepare my carriage. They understood the situation since I was only heading to Baerth Castle. Once I was ready, I set off without bothering to ask for permission—I'm not a child.

In no time, I arrived at Baerth Castle. Since I often visit the Empress, they were already prepared. What surprised me, however, was that it was the Empress's personal maid who greeted me. Her face clearly showed concern.

"Greetings to the Duchess of Audovera," she greeted me.

"How is Her Majesty?" I asked, though I already had a feeling about the answer.

"She is getting worse, Your Grace," Dana's voice held sadness, a clear reflection of her worry."Is it okay to see her?"

"Of course, Your Grace," she said, guiding me to the Empress's room. As we entered, the scent of herbal remedies filled the air, a sign of the treatment the Empress was receiving.

"Your Majesty, Duchess Veronica Audovera is here," Dana announced, and I could hear the soft coughs of Empress Adelaide.

"Veronica?" Her voice was weak, but it made my heart ache as I immediately approached her bedside.

It felt like I hadn't seen her in just a few days, but she had lost so much weight. I noticed the handkerchief she held had blood on it. Had it really gotten this bad?

"Your Majesty..." I held her hand tightly, but it was so cold.

"Veronica, my dearest friend... I don't think I'll be able to visit your new house," she said, and my tears fell freely.

"Please don't say that, Your Majesty," I managed to say, forcing a smile through my tears.

"I would love to talk with you, but... I'm feeling kind of tired."

"Of course, Your Majesty... Dana, please don't leave Her Majesty, okay?" I said to Dana, who was also trying to hold back tears.

"Yes, Duchess," she replied softly.

"Veronica... please take care of Alicia for me," those were the last words I heard from Adelaide before I had to leave her room.

As I walked out, Dana handed me a handkerchief. I quickly took it and composed myself, wiping away the tears before facing the world outside.

Was it already time for this? If there's one thing I wish I could change in this novel, it would be the Empress's death. I've done everything I could to help her, but things never really go the way you want them to.

I guess it's time to go. As I was about to leave, I bumped into Princess Alicia and her maid.

"Greetings, Your Highness Princess Alicia," I greeted, smiling as she beamed back at me.

"I also greet the Duchess of Audovera, Duchess Veronica."

"Oh? That was a perfect greeting, Princess," I clapped my hands in approval.

"Hehehe... I practiced well," she giggled, clearly proud.

"So, where is the princess headed?"

"I came to visit Mother and deliver her favorite flower," she said, showing me the flower she was holding. I glanced at her personal maid, Cara, who seemed a bit more reserved.

"That is so kind of you, Princess. However, Her Majesty is currently asleep. How about you give this lovely flower to Cara, and she will personally deliver it to Her Majesty? What do you think?"

"I guess since I heard Mother needs a lot of sleep," Alicia replied, handing me the flower. "Deliver it later," I told Cara, who nodded.

"Then, Duchess, can we go play again?"

"Of course! How can I refuse such a cute request from this cute princess?" I smiled and gently lifted Princess Alicia, making my way towards the garden. She was only three years old, and I'm not sure if she understood how bad her mother's condition was.

"Duchess, can we do that twirl again?" As soon as we were outside, she asked excitedly.The twirl she was talking about was when I spun her around while holding her. She seemed to enjoy it, but I was getting dizzy from all the spinning.

"Weeee!" I spun her, pretending to fly her around. Luckily, she was light enough that I could keep up with her. Thanks to my past memories as a kindergarten teacher, I knew how to handle kids.

"Do the twirl again, Duchess," she giggled.

"Alicia?" We both looked up when we heard someone call.

"Father!" Alicia immediately ran to the Emperor.

"Are you okay?" I blinked, feeling a bit dizzy from the twirling. My vision blurred for a moment, and I leaned in closer to the person who had spoken to me. But as my vision cleared and I realized who it was, I quickly stepped back.

"Duke? What are you doing here?" I was completely caught off guard by his presence.

"Did you have fun playing with the Duchess?" I heard the Emperor ask Alicia.

"Yes, Father. Playing with the Duchess is always fun," Alicia responded happily. "But who are you with, Father?" she asked, clearly curious since she hadn't met

Duke Henrick before, given that the war had been happening when she was born.

"Ah! This is Duke Henrick Audovera, Princess," the Emperor introduced him.

"I greet Her Royal Highness Princess Alicia Louise Oriviel," Duke Henrick said, bowing to Alicia."Ah! The war hero!" I nodded along with what Alicia said. "The Duchess's husband!" But then, I froze mid-nod when I heard Alicia's next question. "So, when are you and the Duchess going to have a daughter? I want to play with the Duchess' daughter." What in the world was this kid asking?!

"Pfft--" The Emperor couldn't hold back his laughter, most likely because he had taught her to ask that.

"Ha... ha... ha..." I forced out a laugh, feeling awkward. Kids these days are scary. I quickly glanced at my wrist, pretending to check the time. "Oh, look at the time. I think we should get going now," I said, even though I didn't have a watch. Let's just go with the excuse.

After bidding goodbye to the mischievous father and daughter duo, I was finally about to leave when I remembered that I was actually with Duke Henrick. What was he doing here?

"Ah... Duke—"

"Duchess Veronica, it's great to see you here," I was about to ask him when a voice called out to me from behind.

"Ah! Good day, Marquis Staffon," I greeted him.

"Oh, you're with the Duke. Fancy meeting you, Duke Audovera," Marquis Staffon greeted Duke Henrick, who was still wearing his poker face. "It's good that I ran into you, Duchess. I've been meaning to talk with you about this month's crops," he suddenly said, and my eyes widened. I almost forgot about it.

"I'll send you a letter when it's a good time to discuss it, Marquis," I quickly replied. Duke Henrick didn't know about these matters yet.

"Of course, Duchess. Then, I bid you both goodbye," the Marquis said before leaving. Thankfully, he was kind. Now, I just had to figure out how to explain this to the Duke.

"We're going to have a serious talk when we get home," he said, his voice serious. Just as we were about to leave, the carriage I had arrived in pulled up. He opened the door for me and offered his hand.

I had no choice but to accept. He helped me into the carriage, but I was puzzled when he didn't get in himself. "I brought my horse. See you at home, Veronica," he said, closing the carriage door behind me. Then, without another word, he mounted his horse and rode off ahead.

Why was he here again?!

Chapter 8

Here I was, standing in front of Duke Henrick's office door. While I was in the carriage earlier, I kept rehearsing what I was going to say. For a brief moment, I even considered not going home, but then I realized that if I were to run away, I'd need to be prepared. So, in the end, here I am. Let's just explain to him what Marquis Staffon and I arranged last year.

And maybe, just maybe, it's finally time to pass this responsibility to him. Haha!

I was about to knock when the door swung open. It was Evander, and behind him stood the butler. "You may enter now, Duchess," the butler announced before both of them stepped aside and left me alone to face the Duke.

Inside, the Duke was already seated, calmly sipping his tea. I couldn't help but notice the spread of snacks on the table. "Have a seat, Duchess," he instructed, gesturing toward a chair. I took the furthest seat, a solo armchair, putting as much distance between us as possible.

As I sat down, his gaze lingered on me.

Why is he staring? Did I sit weirdly or something?

"I've already been briefed on the arrangements you and Marquis Staffon made regarding the exchange of their crops for our excavated ores," he began, his voice steady and authoritative.Oh? He already knows? Then why am I even here? Wait—he knows about that deal?

"Since the contract is nearing its end, do you plan to extend it or not?" he asked.

The contract he was referring to was the deal I struck with Marquis Staffon last year.

It happened after a series of relentless storms hit Audovera territory. Weeks of heavy rainfall led to devastating floods that wiped out most of the crops. Entire livelihoods were lost, and with half of the territory's food supply coming from those destroyed crops, things looked grim. Even if they replanted once the rains subsided, it would take months before anything could be harvested.

Desperate times call for desperate measures. So when the floods finally receded, I swallowed my pride and went begging to Marquis Staffon.

Marquis Staffon oversees the eastern granary, the largest granary in the empire. Not only do they have vast stretches of farmland, but they're also conveniently spared from storms most of the time. Lucky them. Meanwhile, in Audovera, with barely enough arable land to begin with, everything we plant gets obliterated by floods. Life's just so unfair, isn't it?

Marquis Staffon is the unyielding type—a man of strong responsibility and nobility. At seventy years old, his vast experience made me question how I could possibly persuade him. So, with no other choice, I lowered my pride all the way down.

I made a deal for Marquis Staffon to supply Audovera with crops for a year in exchange for iron ores. Agriculture might not be Audovera's strong suit, but the territory is rich in mines. It wasn't exactly my place to barter the mines or their resources, but hey, desperate times call for desperate measures.

While making that deal, I even knelt in front of him. Yes, knelt.

"How could you kneel so easily? Have you no pride, young lady?" he'd asked, half-amused and half-disapproving.

"Pride won't feed my people, Marquis," I had replied bluntly, not bothered by the softness of the carpet beneath my knees.

That earned a hearty laugh from the old man, and not long after, we formalized the agreement into a contract to make it "legit," as he put it. The deal worked out for both sides anyway; Audovera's iron ores are high-quality, so they weren't losing anything in this arrangement.

But now, back in the present, am I going to extend this contract or not?

Sht!* I had no idea what to do. After a moment of panic, I blurted out, "In my personal opinion, I'd like to change the contract."

Henrick raised a brow. "Why so?"

"Instead of having them continuously supply us with crops, I'd rather ask for something long-term. I want them to send experienced agricultural workers from the east—people who are knowledgeable about farming techniques. They wouldn't need to stay here forever, just long enough to teach the people of Audovera their methods. Our citizens aren't used to farming, and we desperately need expertise to make it sustainable."

There, I laid it all out. A practical and forward-thinking solution, right? Now, if only he wouldn't shoot me down.

The Duke seemed to ponder over my suggestion for a moment. "Alright," he said casually.

I furrowed my brows. "Alright... what?"

"I like your idea," he clarified. "I'll let you handle it since the contract was originally between you and Marquis Staffon."

Wait. What?! That sounded like a lot of work.

"As you wish, Your Grace," I replied reluctantly, biting back a groan. After all, I was the one who started this whole thing.

"Now that we're done with that matter," he said, setting down his teacup and fixing me with a serious gaze. "Let's talk about this divorce nonsense."

EH?!

"Oh, look at the time," I blurted, glancing at my imaginary wristwatch like it was the most natural thing in the world. "Let's discuss this again soon, Your Grace."

Without waiting for his response, I bolted out of the room, practically slamming the door behind me. The second I was outside, I sprinted down the corridor as if my life depended on it. A few startled servants stopped in their tracks, their expressions a mix of confusion and alarm.

But I didn't care. I wasn't about to stick around for that conversation.

Wasn't he supposed to ask for the divorce? Why did it sound like I was the one initiating it? This whole situation was absurd.

Too much had happened today. I needed to rest—desperately.

The sunlight streaming onto my face was what finally woke me. I'd overslept, though I couldn't really call it restful sleep. After tossing and turning all night with thoughts swirling in my head, it was no wonder.

"Come in," I called when a knock sounded at the door. Lucy entered carrying a basin of water for washing, with Butler David following close behind her.

"Good morning, Duchess. You'll be joining His Grace for breakfast today," David informed me.Eh? Stressful this early?

Before I could respond, more maids filed in, arms laden with what I assumed were preparations for the morning.

"We're here to help the Duchess get ready for breakfast," one of them said.

Breakfast? Just breakfast? From the bustle, you'd think I was attending a ball.

After what felt like an eternity of primping, I found myself seated in the grand dining hall. As expected, Duke Henrick was already at the far end of the table.

I took a deep breath and greeted him politely, "Good morning, Your Grace."

He gave me a curt nod as I sat down, eyes briefly scanning the table. The amount of food prepared was absurd—far too much for just the two of us. What a waste.

"Let's eat," he said shortly, signaling the start of the meal.

The silence was deafening, broken only by the clinking of utensils. I focused on eating, trying not to dwell on the oppressive atmosphere. Food, after all, was more important than awkwardness.

Then he dropped a bomb. "Just to let you know, we'll continue our talk later."

I froze mid-chew, silently cursing my fate.

"Yes, I understand, Your Grace," I replied, keeping my tone neutral.

I resumed eating, though my appetite waned. Lucy approached hesitantly, her movements trembling. Her expression wavered like she was debating whether to speak or not.

"What is it?" I asked her quietly, trying to ease her nerves.

Before she could respond, Butler David stepped forward with a grave look on his face.

"Please pardon my sudden interruption, Your Grace," he said.

"What is it, David?" Duke Henrick asked, his tone sharp but calm.

"I regret to inform you that Her Majesty the Empress has passed away."

The words hit me like a punch to the chest. My fork slipped from my hand, clattering loudly onto my plate. Tears pricked my eyes, and before I could stop them, they began falling in steady streams.

No... not her...

Chapter 9

The death of the Empress was inevitable. I already knew it would happen—after all, I'd read about it in the novel. But no amount of foresight could dull the pain of losing someone dear. Her passing sent ripples of grief across the empire, and the entire country mourned the loss of its beloved mother.

The Emperor arranged a beautiful burial ceremony fitting for the late Empress. Though my time with Adelaide had been brief, the moments we shared felt timeless. She had listened to my ramblings with patience and without judgment. If I could turn back time, I would have befriended her long before she became Empress. Instead of wasting my days obsessing over trivial matters, I should have created more memories with her—cherished ones.

It's been three days since the ceremony, and I haven't left my room. The maids are clearly worried. They keep coming by, knocking and calling for me, but I haven't mustered the will to respond. All I've done is curl up in bed, letting my thoughts swirl endlessly. Day turned to night, and the hours blurred together.

Now it's 10 o'clock in the evening. After spending the entire day sleeping, drowsiness refuses to find me. Restless, I decided to take a walk outside. Grabbing a shawl to guard against the chill of the night air, I slipped out of my room quietly, careful not to disturb anyone.

I wandered to the garden, its serenity soothing against the weight of my thoughts. The stillness of the night enveloped me as I looked up at the sky.

The stars shone like scattered diamonds across an endless expanse, and without thinking, I started counting them like some lovesick fool trying to distract herself. "One, two... three..."Adelaide would have teased me for this.

The thought brought a bittersweet smile to my lips.

Meanwhile, Duke Henrick, seated in his study and finishing up a pile of work, glanced out the window. His eyes fell on Veronica, her figure bathed in the soft glow of moonlight as she wandered the garden. It was the first time he had seen her step outside since the passing of the Empress.

He leaned back in his chair, his gaze lingering on her. In his hands were reports detailing the flood incident that struck the Audovera territory a year ago—the same disaster that led to her contract with the East Granary. Yet, as he reviewed the documents, he realized there was something Veronica hadn't shared during their recent discussion.

Her actions during that calamity spoke volumes. When the flood destroyed the homes of countless families, she opened the mansion doors to all who had nowhere to go, offering food and shelter until they could rebuild. The reports also highlighted another detail he hadn't known—how she had ensured that every maid and servant received a generous winter bonus during that time, despite the strain on resources.

Veronica hadn't hosted any extravagant parties or indulged herself with luxuries. Instead, she redirected every coin to those who needed it most. Her selflessness and commitment to the people of Audovera were admirable, especially considering how different she seemed from the woman she had been three years ago.

Henrick placed the papers on his desk, his thoughts weighing heavily on him.

"This isn't the same woman I married," he murmured to himself. There was no disdain in his voice—only a quiet respect and, perhaps, the faintest hint of something deeper.

For the first time in years, the Duke allowed himself to see Veronica not as the Duchess, but as a person—one who had grown and transformed in ways he hadn't expected.

"Achoo!" I sneezed again, the cool night air clearly overstaying its welcome. What was I even doing out here for so long? I should head back inside. As I trudged toward the mansion, it hit me like a brick. "OMG! Adelaide's request!" I smacked my forehead in realization. She made me promise to look after Alicia. What if she haunts me for forgetting?

The next morning, I made my way to the palace, much to Lucy's surprise. "You're back to yourself, Duchess," she remarked, her face lighting up with relief. It was true—I couldn't accomplish anything by wallowing in misery.

I spent the day with Princess Alicia, talking and playing with her. Being around the young princess lifted my spirits. However, it also gave me an earful of the palace gossip, which boiled my blood.

Apparently, several noble families were already holding meetings, each proposing their daughters as candidates for the next Empress. It was outrageous—Adelaide hadn't even been gone for a year! The blatant opportunism was sickening. "If the Emperor dares to take another wife this soon," I muttered under my breath, "I'll shave his head myself."

To distract myself from the swirling anger and sadness, I threw myself into work. Meetings with Marquis Staffon, inspections around the Audovera territory, addressing urgent issues—it kept me busy. This routine went on for a week, leaving little time for anything else.

One afternoon, after a tiring discussion with the farmers, I decided to take a break and stroll around the mansion. While wandering, I noticed three maids huddled together, deep in conversation. Recognizing them as part of Lucy's team, I silently approached, curiosity piqued by their serious expressions.

"It seems like tonight is the night," one of them whispered.

"I know. We must prepare the Duchess," the other replied, her tone urgent.

I raised an eyebrow. Tonight? What's happening tonight? And why do I have no clue about it?I was just about to step forward and ask the maids directly when one of them said something that froze me in place.

"It will be the first night where the Duke and the Duchess will share a bed, so let's make everything perfect," she announced, a hint of excitement in her voice.

I immediately ducked back behind the pillar, my heart racing. What?! Share a bed? What are they even talking about? Panic surged through me. Wait, is this... is this what they mean by marital duty?

Nope. Nope. Nope.

This was definitely my cue to flee. Without wasting another second, I made my way back to my room. Grabbing some money and the trusty robe I used whenever sneaking out of the estate, I took a deep breath. My escape plan was forming.

Before stepping out, I peeked into the hallway, checking for any signs of life. Thankfully, this part of the house was always eerily quiet.

What followed was a chaotic mix of sneaky tactics—walk-run-hide-repeat. I moved through the hallways like a thief in my own home, carefully avoiding every maid and servant. When I reached the kitchen, I breathed a sigh of relief. It was bustling with activity as usual, but no one paid me any attention. To them, I was practically invisible.

And then, a stroke of genius—or desperation—hit me. There was a delivery wagon outside, unloading supplies for the estate. Seeing it as my golden ticket, I quietly climbed into the back and hid among the crates.

Perfect, I thought smugly. This is the best way to escape without anyone noticing. Haha!With my makeshift plan in motion, I hunkered down and prayed I wouldn't get caught.

A couple of hours later...

I could feel it—we were far enough from Audovera territory. With a cautious glance around, I carefully climbed down from the wagon. Thank you for your service, Mr. Deliveryman, I thought with a satisfied smirk as I adjusted my robe.

To blend in more, I removed all my jewelry and tucked them safely in my pockets. Thankfully, I'd chosen a plain dress today—nothing that screamed "noble" or "runaway Duchess."

Looking around, I quickly realized where I was. Ruiledo City. Of all places, I ended up in the so-called City of Nobles. It was a hub where the aristocracy gathered, making it both convenient and dangerous for someone like me. Wrapping the robe tighter around me, I pulled the hood over my head. Safety precautions first—I couldn't risk being recognized.

What made this city so unique was the famous White Tundra Express Train. It was one of the few railways in the empire, and riding it was significantly faster than traveling by carriage.

Without wasting time, I made my way to the ticket booth. Yes, I was paranoid. To cover my tracks, I bought tickets for every single destination the train had. If someone tried to follow me, they'd have no idea where I got off. Genius, right?

Of course, I stuck to economy-class tickets. I didn't want to drain my emergency stash. With tickets in hand, I grabbed some food before boarding the train. It was going to be a long ride, and I needed all the energy I could get.

Inside the economy class, seating was on a first-come, first-served basis. Naturally, I picked the seat furthest in the back—out of sight, out of mind. As soon as I sat down, the train began to move, a smooth and steady rhythm lulling the anxious thoughts in my mind.

I let out a heavy sigh, slumping into the seat. Geez! Why do I feel like some kind of fugitive?

"Excuse me, is this seat taken?"

The soft voice startled me. A woman had approached, her face partially obscured by the hood of her robe. Just like me, she seemed intent on staying inconspicuous. But then my eyes widened.I knew who she was.

What is she doing here?!

MEANWHILE AT THE AUDOVERA ESTATE

The maids were in complete disarray. It had been hours, and not even a shadow of the Duchess could be found. Panic was written all over their faces as they scurried through every corner of the estate. Every room, every corridor, every possible hiding spot had been thoroughly searched, yet there was no sign of Veronica.

Now that they were certain she was gone, dread seeped into their very bones. Someone had to break the news to the Duke—a task none of them wanted to take.

In his office, Duke Henrick was engrossed in his usual stack of documents when the hesitant knock of butler David broke his focus.

"Your Grace," David began, visibly trembling as sweat formed on his brow, "the Duchess... she is nowhere to be found."

The Duke's hand froze mid-motion, the pen in his grip pressing heavily against the paper, nearly tearing it. Though his face remained calm, the atmosphere around him darkened almost instantly. An ominous aura suffused the room, suffocating and cold.

"Summon everyone to the hall," he ordered, his tone icy and devoid of emotion.

David gulped audibly and quickly bowed. "Y-yes, Your Grace!"

The tension in the estate reached a boiling point as every staff member assembled in the grand hall within minutes. Fear was etched into their faces, knowing full well the wrath that awaited them. The Duke's steps echoed menacingly as he descended the staircase, his piercing gaze sweeping over the cowering servants.

"Find her," he commanded, his voice like a blade slicing through the heavy silence. "Search every corner of this empire if you must. But bring the Duchess back to me."

No one dared to hesitate. The staff scattered like leaves in a storm, driven by both fear and determination.

The Duke's jaw tightened as he turned toward the windows, gazing out into the dark horizon. Veronica, wherever you've run off to... I'll find you.

Chapter 10

I was taken aback when I recognized the woman who had asked the question. Why is Irene here?

"Duchess Veronica Audovera?!" she exclaimed. I quickly pulled her down into the empty seat beside me. "Ssshh!"

"I'm sorry, but why are you alone, Duchess? Is the Duke not with you?" she whispered, her eyes wide with curiosity.

"I kind of ran away, so you'd better lower your voice," I whispered back, my tone soft but firm.She seemed taken aback at first, but then her face lit up with a small, excited smile. "What a coincidence. I also ran away from the temple!" she said, practically glowing with giddiness. What's going on with the heroine? This side of her was so unexpected. I always remembered Irene as the delicate, docile type, the one described in the novel as incapable of breaking even a single plate... or was I remembering that wrong?

"But why did you run away, Your Grace?" she asked, her voice filled with genuine concern. I found myself gazing out the window, lost in thought, as I struggled to find an answer.

"I feel suffocated," I admitted softly, the weight of my emotions pressing down on me. Confusion, frustration ... everything was a tangled mess in my mind. The real reason, though? The bed-sharing situation. That's what really drove me to this point. "And please, just call me Veronica," I added, wanting to shed the formalities for a moment of clarity.

"Really? Then, please call me Irene," she replied, her voice warm and cheerful.

I smiled faintly, but my thoughts still lingered on the storm that was brewing inside me. "What about you? What made you run away from the temple?" I asked, genuinely curious about her reasons.

She sighed deeply. "The temple has been making me do all kinds of work. I haven't had a proper rest since coming back from the war," she explained, and I couldn't help but notice the dark circles under her eyes. She looked utterly exhausted. I thought I was the only one feeling this worn out.

"This may be a bit sudden, but I'd really like to become close to you, Duchess Veronica," she added with a hopeful smile. I frowned at her words.

"Close to me? Aren't you aware of the rumors about me? The crazy lady of high society?" I couldn't help but ask.

"I've heard those rumors, but aren't they from the past? What matters now is who Duchess Veronica is today. I really admire you, especially for what you did during the war. Did you know I coined the name Angel of War for you?" she said, and I couldn't help but gape at her. "Angel of War?" I asked, bewildered. "I didn't even participate in the war," I added, feeling a bit confused.

Irene smiled brightly.

An hour passed as she explained to me how I came to be known as the Angel of War. It all stemmed from the secret shipments of war supplies I sent over the course of three years. I had done it because of the knowledge I had gained from reading the novel. I remembered that the enemy always targeted supply depots with bombs, and that left the soldiers without food and medical supplies. The result? Countless casualties.

"We were in despair when they destroyed the fort. So many knights were injured, and there were only nine priests, including myself, left to help. Healing the injured was draining. I honestly thought I was going to collapse from exhaustion. Supplies would take weeks to arrive. But then, a miracle happened. War supplies arrived the very next day. You may not realize it, but those supplies saved countless lives, Duchess. Because of that, we were able to keep going, and not a single life was lost. We are all incredibly grateful to you."

I felt a rush of emotions as her words sank in. I had never imagined that something I did, something so small and secretive, had such a profound impact. I was silent for a moment, the weight of it all pressing down on me.

I scratched my head in confusion. That was supposed to be a secret! How did they figure out it was me? I was so careful to make sure it came from the palace! Wait, does that mean the Duke knows about this too?!

Irene continued telling her story, and I was getting embarrassed because it was all about me. Shouldn't this be about the Duke? I mean, they're the protagonists. "How about the Duke?" I asked, frowning when she paused.

"What about him?" she replied, as though my question was strange. Something felt off.

"What do you think of the Duke?" I pressed, and she seemed to think for a moment.

"Truthfully, I find Duke Henrick... scary," she said. Huh? In the novel, he was described as a sweet, caring person. What is this "scary" stuff she's talking about? "Wherever the Duke is, there's a bloodbath. Literally. I saw him fight once, and I nearly fainted. That's why I only spoke to him when there was a meeting during the war," she added, hugging herself as if she was shivering from the memory.

Seriously, something's not right here!

I didn't expect to get along with her this well. It felt like I was just chatting with a friend. We talked for hours—well, mostly Irene did the talking. She even mentioned that every day she prays for there to never be another war. If there were, she'd leave the temple for good.

Why is she considering rebelling against the temple? Was the war that traumatic for them? Maybe it was the exhaustion catching up with her because Irene eventually fell asleep. I glanced out the window, watching the scenery pass by. It had been hours since I ran away from the Audovera estate. They must have noticed by now.

Pfft. There's no way they can find me, right? The Duke has no idea where I built my house. It'll be my first time seeing it too, and I'm excited. Especially the pool! Haha! I felt my eyes grow heavier and realized I was starting to doze off. Time for a quick nap.

"This is the last stop, ladies," the conductor's voice suddenly jolted me awake. I realized the train had come to a complete stop. My God! What was supposed to be a quick nap turned into a long, deep sleep. Did we really sleep through the entire night?

"T-thank you," I quickly woke Irene, who was still beside me. Wait, where was she going? "Irene?"

"Veronica?" she murmured, then looked around, clearly disoriented. "Where are we?"

"We're at the last stop." We rushed to get off the train. The conductor was clearly annoyed with how slow we were moving. Haha! "By the way, Irene, where were you headed?"

"Well, now that you mention it, I don't really have a specific place to go. I just got on the train," she said, scratching her head. I paused for a moment, thinking.

"Do you want to come with me?" I asked, and her face instantly lit up.

"Can I really?" she asked eagerly.

"Yes."

"Yay! But where do we go? We're in a rural area."

"There's a small, quiet town nearby called Charringtown. It's peaceful and safe there. A perfect place to get away from everything. Shall we head to the market first?" I suggested as we started walking together.

Of course, we first stopped by the market to buy food and even picked up a few clothes. I noticed Irene didn't have any extra clothes with her. She only had a small bag, much like me. We both ran away without thinking to pack properly.

After shopping, we quickly made our way to the house I was talking about. We rented a wagon since we bought a lot, and the house was far from the market. It took us at least two hours to get there.

Irene's jaw dropped when she saw the house. I felt the same way. Were rest houses always this huge around here? It seemed almost too big for something my father had built.

"Was there always a big house in this remote area?" Irene mumbled in disbelief.

"I actually own this place. It's a house I asked my father to build," I replied, and after we got everything inside and settled the rent for the wagon, I grabbed Irene to give her a tour. "Irene, could you keep this house a secret? Only my father and I know about it."

"Of course, Veronica. But this house design is really unique," she said, and I couldn't help but smile. I designed it myself, after all. I felt proud. I then pulled Irene to the back of the house where the pool was.

"Whoa. What's this?" she asked in awe.

"This is a swimming pool. I requested this when they built the house," I explained.

"It's like a giant bathtub. Wait, are you really going to swim in it?"

"Well, of course. By the way, you can use the other room on the second floor," I added, glad I had asked my father to build an extra room. I was surprised when Irene suddenly hugged me, thanking me. I just chuckled. Irene was so cute.

Before we jumped into the pool, we decided to have something to eat first. So here we were now in the kitchen. Luckily, there were already supplies here. "Thank you, Father," I whispered, grateful.

"There's a rice grain here," Irene said, showing me a jar full of rice. Oh my god, rice. Well, eating rice in this world isn't exactly common. I did ask my father for some, but I didn't expect him to actually find rice. People here don't typically eat it.

I made my way to the rice and started cooking it. While waiting for it to cook, I began preparing the dish. Since we were both hungry, I decided to make something easy to cook. Irene helped by peeling the garlic and onion. I then mixed everything in a pot. Luckily, there were condiments here already. Thank you so much, Father.

After about 30 minutes, my stomach started growling. I began serving the food, and Irene helped me with the plates. "I didn't know that the Duchess of Audovera cooks," she said, amazed.

We started eating together. "This is actually the first time I've cooked for others," I said. Actually, it's the first time since I remembered my past life. Plus, this was the first chance I've had to cook. I took a bite of rice with the dish, and suddenly, I felt a lump in my throat. I missed rice so much, and this... it was just perfect.

"Irene? Why are you crying?" I asked, surprised.

"This is so delicious, Veronica. What is this?" she asked, tears in her eyes.

"It's pork adobo," I replied.

We continued eating. I don't know what happened, but the rice was all gone, and we were both full. Irene even asked me how to make adobo. Haha! She kept saying it should be the national dish here. Afterward, we went swimming.

This was the vacation we needed. Two days passed by so quickly. We made all sorts of dishes. I even introduced Irene to chicken tinola and pork sinigang. Haha!

Currently, I was sitting by the pool, enjoying the peaceful atmosphere. These past two days had been perfect. I wished it could stay this way forever. What should I cook next? Do we still have enough food stocked? I was lost in thought about what to cook when Irene rushed toward me, panicked.

"Veronica! Veronica! We have a problem!" she said, breathless as she approached.

"What is it—" I froze, standing up in shock as I saw Duke Henrick standing there.

WHAT IS HE DOING HERE?!

Chapter 11

"There are hundreds of people here in the house, yet no one saw the Duchess escape?" The servants in the hall trembled, their fear palpable, as they had never witnessed Duke Henrick this enraged before.

Days passed, and Duke Henrick relentlessly searched through the entire Audovera estate and even ventured beyond its borders, refusing to stop. Evanders, his most trusted right-hand man, grew increasingly concerned. The Duke hadn't rested or slept in days.

It wasn't until the emperor summoned him that the Duke finally received vital information regarding the Duchess's whereabouts.

Without hesitation, the Duke departed for the palace to meet the emperor.

"Duke Audovera, this is probably the fastest you've arrived after being summoned," the emperor remarked.

"Where is she?" the Duke asked, his voice cold and direct.

"Straight to the point, are we? But I must say, I'm curious. Why did Veronica suddenly run away?" The emperor's tone shifted when he heard the Duke refer to the Duchess by her name.

"That's Duchess Audovera to you," Duke Henrick corrected him sharply.

The emperor chuckled, though his amusement quickly faded at the sight of the Duke's stern expression.

"Hahahaha... Anyway, I also heard that the saintess ran away. What a coincidence, don't you think? Hahaha... heh... ehem!" The emperor's laughter faltered as he noticed the seriousness in the Duke's demeanor.

"The Duchess was last seen in Ruiledo City, aboard the White Tundra Express Train. I'm not sure exactly where she went, as she bought tickets for all the stops. However, I did receive an unusual building permit from Marquis Cosimo a few years ago, and as far as I recall, it was for a location in Charringtown—" Before the emperor could finish, the Duke stormed out of the room.

Emperor Darius rubbed his forehead, exasperated. "The Audovera couple sure is entertaining..."

When Duke Henrick arrived at the express train station, he immediately rented the entire train to ensure a faster journey.

Because the train never made any stops, they arrived in Charringtown in no time. The Duke brought only a small group of knights with him. They scoured the small town, searching for any leads. It wasn't until a delivery man pointed them toward a peculiar house that they found their first clue.

Following the directions given, the Duke approached the uniquely described house. As he raised his hand to knock on the door, it swung open, and to his shock, the missing saintess stood before him.

The look of surprise on their faces was unmistakable. The Duke momentarily wondered if the emperor had played a trick on him, but before he could process further, Irene suddenly shouted, "Veronica!"

It's only been two days. How on earth did he find me so quickly? What the heck!?

Whoever gave away the location of this place better be ready to face my wrath. Seriously!I began to panic as Duke Henrick started making his way toward me. I was about to run, but before I could, I slipped and fell right into the pool.

"Veronica!" I heard Duke Henrick call my name as he jumped in after me. But damn, water rushed into my ears.

'Do I have a birthmark on my butt? I should check that later.'

"Ahh... Duke?" I looked at where the Duke had landed, but he was just floating in the water.

"Duke?" I called out again, but when there was no response, I immediately swam toward him.

"Duke?" I gently slapped his face, but then I froze, my hands pressing against his forehead... it was burning hot.

'Is he sick?'

I quickly scanned the area. It was clear that we were alone. Who could I possibly ask for help? I dragged his unconscious body to the side of the pool and pushed him toward the edge.

I ran to the gazebo and grabbed my towel. Once I had it, I hurried back to him, wrapping it around his body. I was struggling, exhausted, because I wasn't strong enough to carry him easily. How was I supposed to get him inside? Should I just roll him over?

With no other choice, I managed to piggyback him to my room since it was the closest. I didn't know how long it took me to get him there, but it felt like forever.

I was struggling under his weight, especially with the height difference between us, not to mention the heavy breaths coming from him, which made it even harder.

When we finally made it to my room, I dropped him onto the bed, then stretched to relieve my aching back.

Before anything else, I changed out of my wet clothes. Afterward, I looked for something he could wear. I couldn't leave him in wet clothes—he would get sicker. But why did he have a fever in the first place?

I had searched through every available item of clothing in the house, but couldn't find any men's clothes or anything that might fit him.

My eyes landed on my pink pajamas. It wasn't just pink—it was hot pink. Since it was stretchy, it should fit him, right?

I grabbed them, thinking it would be better than letting him stay soaked. But now the problem was... how the heck was I supposed to change him?

I checked his face to make sure he was actually asleep. Fortunately, he was out cold. With shaky hands, I began unbuttoning his shirt.

This was the most nerve-wracking thing I'd ever done in my life. Why did it feel like I was committing a crime? I was just removing his wet clothes!

But then I almost fainted when I saw his abs. How could he have such a perfectly sculpted body?Is this some kind of torture?!

Slap

I slapped myself. This was the first time I'd seen a man's naked body in this life. That must be why I was so startled. But seriously... he had a perfectly toned body.

I quickly slapped myself a few more times, trying to shake off the embarrassment, before managing to change his shirt. But now, a new problem emerged—how the heck was I supposed to change his pants?!

I could leave them and just let them dry, but he might feel uncomfortable. And what if his condition worsens? He might blame me.

After a moment of contemplation, I decided to go ahead and remove his pants. After all, he wasn't aware of anything. I could hang them up to dry and once they were dry, I'd put them back on him—just like nothing ever happened. Haha!

I made the sign of the cross before I reached for his belt. To all the saints and angels, please don't let him wake up right now.

Slowly, I started to undo his belt, but then suddenly...

"V-Veronica?"

My heart skipped a beat as I looked up. Duke Henrick was wide-eyed, staring at me with shock in his eyes, while my hand was still gripping his belt.

"AAAHHH!!!"

I couldn't help but scream in mortification.

Chapter 12

I quickly yanked my hand away from his belt and bolted out of the room, my heart racing as I leaned against the door once I was outside.

My heart was pounding so fast. "Hoo!" I muttered to myself. He should be changing on his own now that he's awake, right? I should focus on preparing his meal instead.

I walked toward the kitchen, relieved that we still had some stock. I could make chicken soup for him. It's easy to cook, easy to eat, and packed with the nutrients he needs right now.

It took me nearly an hour to prepare it, and by then, it was already lunchtime. I needed to bring it to Duke Henrick before it got cold.

I took a deep breath before opening the door again. Damn it! Let's do this! I pushed the food trolley into the room and walked over to his bed.

He was still fast asleep, thankfully. I noticed that he was already wearing the hot-pink pajama I'd given him earlier.

Thank goodness!

I picked up the clothes scattered on the floor. Since I didn't have any servants here, I was the one who would have to wash them. Now, I faced another problem.

I looked back at Duke Henrick's face. Damn it! He's too handsome! It's not fair. He's sick, but he's still incredibly good-looking—what the hell am I thinking? I should wake him up.

But how the heck do I wake him up without him getting mad?

"Your Grace?" I softly called out to him. "Your Grace?" Should I feed him while he's still asleep? It's risky if he wakes up suddenly.

And considering the embarrassment from earlier, I was hesitant. "Your Grace?" I said again, trying to get his attention. "Wake up before the soup gets cold!"

I poked his cheek, but suddenly, he moved, and my finger slipped into his nose.

Seriously, Veronica? What else are you going to do to him?

"V-Veronica?" His voice was groggy, and I froze.

I carefully helped him sit up.

"Your Grace, I'm sorry for waking you, but you need to eat something," I explained, placing the tray in front of him.

I noticed that he was just staring at the soup. Was he thinking I poisoned it?

"It's chicken soup. I cooked it myself, but don't worry, I guarantee it's edible, Your Grace," I reassured him. But he was still staring at it, unmoving. Did he really not want it? He glanced at me and then at the spoon.

What now? Don't tell me—

"Perhaps y-you want me to feed you?" I asked hesitantly, Please say no, you bastard! You just have a fever, you're not crippled!

I almost had a heart attack when Duke Henrick gave me that look, like I was some abandoned dog on the street. What is that look supposed to mean?

But since I felt guilty, I just grabbed the spoon and tried to feed him. I did my best to keep a poker face, but I was still so nervous.

I scooped some of the chicken soup and blew on it to cool it down a bit since it was still hot. Duke Henrick just kept staring at my face, and I could feel the pressure building up.

I wanted to close my eyes while feeding him to avoid the awkwardness, but that would make me look ridiculous. After a few minutes, I finally finished feeding him. It should've been quick, but my mind was still racing over the embarrassing things I had done earlier.

Because I was so self-conscious of his gaze, I accidentally left the spoon in his mouth after he took a bite. I couldn't decide whether to laugh at my awkwardness or to be terrified because he suddenly furrowed his brows.

I started cleaning up the food after giving him his drink. I was about to leave when he suddenly grabbed my hand.

"Duke?" I asked, surprised.

He handed me the cup he had been drinking from.

Ah, so he just wanted me to take the cup. Ha-ha! I grabbed it and put it on the food trolley. I was about to leave again, but then he stopped me once more.

"Where are you going?" he asked, his tone soft but insistent.

"I have to clean the dishes and...," I glanced at the food trolley and then back to his wet clothes from earlier, "...wash your clothes?"

He seemed to think for a moment before suddenly standing up.

"Wait. Your Grace?" he asked, and I froze.

"I'll help you," he said, and I immediately tried to stop him.

"No, Your Grace. You don't have to. I can do this on my own, plus you're sick," I firmly told him.

"But--"

"No buts! If you want to help, then why don't you lie down and rest?" I insisted, gently guiding Duke Henrick back onto the bed and wrapping him in the blanket. I touched his forehead with the back of my hand to check his temperature. "See? You're still warm," I added. "You need to sleep."

As I was about to pull my hand away, he took it again and placed it against his cheek.

"I will sleep, but you are not going anywhere," he said, closing his eyes.

"But--"

"No buts, Veronica," he interrupted.

I tried to pull my hand away, but his grip tightened. Why is he so strong?

I gave up, letting my hand remain where it was. It's probably my fault he's sick anyway. I'll just wait for him to fall asleep completely.

I sat on the side of the bed and stared at his face. This was the first time I'd seen him like this—weak. His face was flushed, and sweat dotted his forehead. But, damn, why does he still look so attractive?

What happened to your mantra, Veronica?

There should be no more lingering feelings. You've moved on. You no longer have any feelings for this man.

But who am I fooling? I've spent half my life loving him. There's no way those feelings will vanish that easily.

I may have tried to forget him over the past three years, but the feelings I buried rushed back as soon as I saw his face.

I didn't even realize I'd started crying. A bitter smile crossed my face as I gazed at the sleeping Duke Henrick.

I noticed his grip on my hand had loosened, so I carefully withdrew it.

I stood up slowly, checking his forehead one last time. He wasn't as warm anymore. Before I left the room, I leaned down and kissed him on the forehead, then quietly left with the trolley.Once he wakes up, I should properly ask him about the divorce.

I left the room, but I didn't abandon Duke Henrick. It's my house, after all.

I just needed to step out to do some cleaning—wash the dishes, do the laundry. I didn't want chores piling up. Haha! Like I always do this.

It's just that there are no servants today.

After I washed up and did Duke's laundry, I checked on him again to see how his temperature was.

It wasn't as high as before. He probably just needed more rest. What did he even do?

Once I checked on Duke Henrick, I stepped out again, pretending to clean around the house until I got tired.

I rested by the pool and had a snack as the day slowly turned into evening.

I decided to take a shower because I felt like it, and then I headed to the room where Duke was resting. I was just going to ask what he wanted for dinner.

Did he prefer boiled sweet potatoes or boiled potatoes? That's all I had in the kitchen. Crazy! When I walked into the room, I immediately looked for the person who should've been resting on the bed. "Your Grace?" I closed the door to search for him when suddenly, someone hugged me from behind.

"Veronica," he whispered into my ear, sending shivers down my spine.

"Y-your Grace?" I tried to break free and face him, but he wouldn't let me go. "W-wait, how are you feeling?"

"I'm all better now, Veronica," he answered, letting go of me and turning me to face him. "Now, let's go home."

Huh? I instinctively stepped back.

"Actually, there is something I want to ask of you," I started.

"Ask?"

"Yes, Your Grace. Due to my selfishness and childishness, you were pressured to marry me by my father. What I want is your forgiveness for my selfishness. I am truly sorry for all the inconveniences I have caused you,"

I took a deep breath, my eyes downcast. I was afraid that if I looked at him, I might lose myself again.

"I want to make up for everything I did wrong. Starting with you," and then I couldn't help but flashback to all the mischief I caused before.

"Is this why you're preparing for a divorce?" I looked at him in shock. Wait, how did he know?"H-how did you—" I stepped back when I noticed he was moving closer.

"Do you still love me, Veronica?"

"What?" I stepped back as Duke Henrick continued to approach me.

"Even if you don't love me anymore..." He kept coming closer, and I didn't notice I had backed up until I felt the bed against my legs, causing me to sit down unexpectedly. "Then I'll make you fall for me again. However long it takes," he added, his voice soft yet determined. Before I could react, he leaned down and kissed me on the lips.

"You are mine, Veronica," he whispered, his eyes intense. "I'll make sure you have nowhere else to go but stay with me... forever."

I froze, heart racing, as he gently lifted me, guiding me to lie down on the bed. "Your Grace..." My words trailed off as I felt his lips trail down my neck, a sensation that made my breath catch.His hands moved carefully, as though making sure I was comfortable. "If you want my forgiveness," he murmured, "then let's leave the divorce behind us."

I couldn't believe it. This wasn't what I had imagined. It felt like a dream, but with every touch, it became real.

"Your Grace..." I said softly, my voice quivering. His hands were gentle as he explored, making sure I felt safe. I closed my eyes, feeling vulnerable but strangely cared for.

He paused for a moment, studying me. "You're beautiful, Veronica," he said, and my heart fluttered.

"Tell me if anything hurts," he added, his concern for me clear.

I nodded, though the emotions I was feeling were overwhelming. "It's... it's fine," I whispered, trying to steady myself.

"Then I'll go slowly," he promised, his voice gentle as he continued, making sure I was comfortable every step of the way.

His care and tenderness took me by surprise, and for the first time in a long while, I let myself feel safe in his arms. The pain I felt was overshadowed by the warmth of his presence and the love he was offering, even in this vulnerable moment.

As I looked into his eyes, I felt a rush of emotions—memories of our time together, the pain of the past, and the hope for a future together. "I love you, Henrick," I whispered, my voice full of sincerity.

His lips curved into a soft smile. "I love you too, Veronica," he answered, his words steady and full of emotion as he held me close.

Chapter 13

Before the war, when I first met Veronica, I couldn't say I was enamored with her at first glance. She had a reputation, one that many would rather avoid, but there was something undeniably captivating about her. Even with all the gossip and rumors swirling around her, I found myself intrigued.

She was rash, fiery, and unafraid to speak her mind—traits that didn't exactly make her popular with the high society women, but somehow, they made her even more interesting to me. In truth, I enjoyed watching her fight for my attention, even if it was a bit... chaotic at times. There was a charm to her boldness that I couldn't ignore. Maybe that's why, when her father proposed the idea of marriage to her, I didn't reject it outright. A part of me admired her spirit, and I thought perhaps it was time to make my own decision, regardless of the society's whispers.

Our marriage came sooner than I expected. Honestly, I wasn't sure how it would go. There were many things I wasn't ready for, least of all the weight of what marriage meant. But despite her sometimes rash behavior and our differences, I found myself fond of Veronica. I even found her cute in her own way, despite the chaos she often stirred up.

Then came the war. It was a time of unrest, and after our wedding, being thrust into battle was the last thing I wanted. I'd barely gotten used to my new role as a husband, and now I was supposed to leave everything behind to fight for my kingdom. I had no choice but to obey orders, though the anger I felt toward being sent away was something I couldn't hide.

During the war, I was consumed with thoughts of Veronica, and to my surprise, those thoughts became a source of comfort. The thought of her back home kept me going, even as I faced the harsh realities of war. I knew she was strong, but I couldn't help but worry. Had I made the right choice marrying her? What would happen to her without me there? But as the days turned into weeks, and weeks into months, my thoughts of Veronica shifted. It wasn't just worry anymore; I began to feel something deeper.

When I learned about the things Veronica had done for Audovera during my absence, my heart shifted in a way I didn't expect. The town, our people—she had put her own reputation aside and worked tirelessly to help those in need. She wasn't just the rash, hot-headed woman I had married; she was someone who had grown, someone who had changed for the better. My admiration for her deepened. I hadn't realized it at the time, but somewhere in the distance, I had started to fall in love with the woman she had become.

I returned home to find her... different. Not in a bad way, but I could sense the change. The woman I had left behind was no longer the same one who greeted me when I returned. She had grown stronger, more confident, more compassionate. But when I learned that she was considering a divorce, panic set in. I couldn't let her go, not after everything she had done, not after everything we had been through together. The thought of losing her was something I wasn't prepared for.

Now, as I stand here, unsure of how to approach her, I realize just how much I care for her. I've always found it difficult to express my feelings—one of my many flaws—but now it seems that I've taken too long. Veronica, despite everything, had been there for me, for our people, and I can no longer stand by and let her think that I don't see her efforts. I have to tell her how I feel, before it's too late.

I lay in bed now, unable to move. I was dressed and ready, but Henrick had taken care of everything. He insisted we were heading back to the Duchy today.

I had no choice. First, I couldn't move—Henrick had injured me last night. He had lost control, and as a result, my hip was broken. Secondly, the topic of the divorce was strictly off-limits.

"Veronica?" Henrick's voice brought me back to reality. "We're going home." I nodded in silence, not trusting my voice.

Because of my injury, Henrick carried me. As he did, I covered my face with my hands, feeling the eyes of the Audovera knights on us. Their stares were too much to bear.

This was incredibly embarrassing.

Henrick carried me all the way to the train. I made sure to hide my face, but at least he had rented the entire carriage, so no one could see us. We reached Audovera in no time, and upon our arrival at the castle, a whole group of maids and servants was waiting for us. They were smiling, but there was something off about their smiles. It made me feel even more self-conscious, so I kept my face hidden as Henrick carried me toward his room.

"Starting now, you'll be staying in my room," he announced, and then he left the room for a moment.

I wanted to roll around on the bed, but the pain in my lower body made it impossible.

It wasn't long before the family doctor arrived, prescribing various medicines and ointments. Lucy, the head maid, entered next, offering me tea.

"Welcome back, Duchess. As requested by the Duke, here is the pain-relieving tea and special ointment. Please ring the bell if you need any further assistance," she said. After placing the tea and ointment on the bedside table, she left the room.

"Veronica," Henrick's voice broke through my thoughts as he returned. He took the tea and helped me drink it, his gaze full of guilt. I couldn't help but feel a twinge of frustration.

"I'm sorry, Veronica," he said, his voice strained. "I should've controlled myself last night. To make it up to you, I'll help you apply this ointment."

I looked at him, puzzled. "I'm alright, but what's the ointment for?" I asked, unsure of what to expect.

To my surprise, Henrick looked down, his face slightly flushed. "It's for... your private part," he admitted, his voice low.

I felt a flush rise in my cheeks, but I could see the sincerity in his eyes. Despite the awkwardness, I could sense that he truly regretted what had happened. This wasn't just about the physical pain; there was a deeper layer of care in his actions now.

Though I wasn't ready to fully process everything, one thing was clear: Henrick's feelings had shifted, and I wasn't sure whether that was a blessing or a curse.

Chapter 14

Two weeks passed... and Henrick made sure I never left the room.

"I just want to make sure you're fully healed before you go back to work," he kept saying as an excuse.

Even though my hip was already completely healed. In fact, I managed to move around a bit the other day.

"Duchess, here's your lunch," Lucy announced as she placed my meal on the table before leaving the room.

I watched her set it down before heading towards the food, but the smell hit me, and I immediately backed away. I ran straight to the bathroom and threw up.

This... this is something I haven't told Henrick yet. He's been so busy lately. He's been coming home late, and honestly, it feels like everyone here has their hands full.

I returned to the bed, but before lying down, I had the food brought to me. I lay there, unable to find any comfort.

"Duchess, a gift has arrived from Priestess Irene Theano," a maid said.

"Leave it there. Thanks, Lucy," I replied, as she left the room. I looked at the gift. Was it my birthday? Why would Irene be sending me a gift?

"Congratulations, Duchess Veronica Audovera, from your friend, Irene Theano."

Huh? Does she know...?

When I opened the gift, my eyes widened. "Isn't this bridal underwear?" Wait, why on earth is Irene giving me something like this?

I quickly hid the gift away. What is Irene thinking?

The next morning, I woke up to the sounds of Lucy and the other maids moving around. To my surprise, there were seven other maids in the room.

"Good morning, Duchess," they greeted in unison.

What's going on here?

"By the way, where is Henrick?" I asked Lucy as the maids continued helping me get ready. I was confused because they were going all out with my appearance.

"The Duke is currently at the palace, Duchess," Lucy answered.

"Okay? But why am I wearing this overly designed white gown?" I asked, noticing the extravagant outfit they were dressing me in. Aside from the thick makeup, the gown was incredibly elaborate.

"The Duke wants you to deliver this letter," Lucy explained, handing me the envelope. I looked at it and saw that it was an invitation for breakfast with the emperor. Huh? Is this really happening?A few hours later, I found myself in a carriage on my way to the palace. Before long, we arrived. A group of maids greeted me, and I was handed a bouquet of flowers.

"Excuse me, but where exactly are we going?" I asked the maids, but they only smiled in response.

I thought this was supposed to be a breakfast gathering, but why did it feel like we were heading straight for the throne room? Were we going to eat there?

By the time we reached the large doors of the throne room, my questions went unanswered. What was going on?

"Duchess of Audovera, you may now enter the throne room," said the knight standing guard outside.

"Okay?" I replied, my confusion growing.

When the doors opened, I gasped in surprise. The room was filled with people, all clapping and cheering for me.

The moment I stepped into the throne room, my jaw dropped. The decorations were stunning—flowers, silken drapes, and candles lined the walls. It looked like someone was getting married."Veronica, my daughter," a familiar voice called out.

I turned to see none other than my father. "F-Father? What are you doing here?"

"Well, I couldn't miss my daughter's wedding," he said with a sly smile, which only deepened my confusion.

"You have another daughter?" I asked, dumbfounded.

"It's your wedding, Veronica. The Duke planned everything," he replied before gently turning me to face the gathered crowd. My eyes traveled down the aisle until they landed on Henrick, standing at the end, looking dashing beyond words.

My heart skipped several beats. My father started walking me down the aisle, and I felt like an absolute fool for not realizing what was happening sooner. Before I knew it, I was standing face-to-face with Henrick.

"Am I dreaming?" I blurted out, earning a chuckle from him.

"This is real, Veronica," he said warmly, taking my hand and kissing it with such tenderness that my chest tightened.

"But... aren't we already married?"

"Yes," he said with a small smile, "but we never had a proper wedding."

A wave of emotions surged through me—shock, joy, disbelief. My throat tightened as tears prickled at the edges of my eyes. So this is why he's been so busy lately... he was planning all of this.

Henrick turned us toward the emperor, who stood waiting with an almost mischievous grin plastered across his face. I blinked. Was the emperor... officiating our wedding?

The ceremony began, with the emperor speaking in his deep, regal voice. But my focus wasn't on him. I barely heard his words because Henrick leaned closer to me and murmured softly, "Knowing that you are beside me... I am truly happy."

A smile crept across my lips, warmth spreading through my chest. "We will both be beside you forever, Henrick," I replied gently.

Henrick froze for a moment, his eyes searching mine, and then realization dawned on his face. The depth of my words had struck him—I wasn't speaking only for myself.

Before I could say anything else, Henrick pulled me into a kiss. My eyes widened as our lips met, right in the middle of the emperor's speech.

"We're not in that part yet!" the emperor's voice boomed, sounding both startled and exasperated. A collective gasp rose from the crowd as Henrick deepened the kiss, ignoring every ounce of decorum.

It wasn't a quick kiss, either. It was long, passionate, and full of all the things Henrick rarely said out loud. It was as though he was pouring all his emotions into this one act, right in front of everyone.

By the time we pulled apart, my face was burning, and I could see people whispering and giggling. The emperor looked absolutely scandalized.

"Shall we finish the ceremony before your enthusiasm gets the better of you, Duke?" the emperor said, raising an eyebrow.

Henrick laughed, unrepentant, and I couldn't help but laugh along with him.

The rest of the ceremony went by in a blur. My thoughts swirled with disbelief and happiness. By the time the emperor pronounced us husband and wife, the room erupted in applause.

As we turned to face the crowd, Henrick whispered into my ear, "You'll never have to doubt how much I love you, Veronica. Not today, not ever."

My heart felt like it could burst with happiness.

Later, the kiss became the hot topic of the empire. Some were scandalized, others amused, but honestly, who cared? As far as I was concerned, it was perfect—just like Henrick.

Chapter 15

Two years had passed and my life had taken a decidedly unexpected turn. As a mother to twins, Dominic and Dahlia, and a surrogate guardian to Princess Alicia, my days were filled with both chaos and joy.

Walking through the grand halls of the imperial palace, Dominic nestled snugly in my arms while Dahlia toddled ahead, her laughter echoing off the marble walls.

"Dahlia, wait for Mama," I called gently, though she was already racing toward Princess Alicia's chamber, her little legs moving faster than I thought possible.

Alicia, hearing the commotion, flung open the doors with an excited cry. "Duchess Veronica! You're here!"

I smiled warmly as she darted out, nearly colliding with Dahlia, who squealed in delight. "Careful, Alicia," I teased. "You don't want to knock over your future best friend."

Alicia giggled and scooped up Dahlia in her arms. "Oh, I've missed you!" she said, twirling with my daughter as Dominic watched them both with an amused coo.

"Don't worry, Dominic," I murmured, pressing a kiss to his downy hair. "Your turn will come soon enough."

After a bit of playful chaos, I settled Dominic into the arms of a maid and let Alicia lead Dahlia to the plush rug in the center of the room, where a pile of toys awaited. The sight of the three girls—Alicia, Dahlia, and a doll—sharing a "tea party" tugged at my heart.

"She loves the twins," a soft voice said from behind me.

I turned to see Irene, clad in the familiar white robes of her priestess duties. Her presence always brought a sense of calm, though today there was a slight edge to her expression.

"And they adore her," I replied, patting the seat beside me. Irene hesitated before sitting down, smoothing her robes.

"You look exhausted," she noted with a faint smile.

"Twins will do that to you," I replied with a laugh. "But I wouldn't trade it for anything." I paused, studying her. "And you? How are things at the temple?"

She sighed, brushing a loose strand of hair from her face. "Demanding, as always. But at least my frequent visits to the palace offer a... change of pace."

Her tone was nonchalant, but there was a flicker of something in her eyes—something unresolved. Before I could press her further, a voice from outside the chamber broke our conversation.

"Irene, running from me again?"

We both turned toward the sound. It was the emperor, leaning casually against the doorframe, his dark eyes glinting with mischief.

Irene's lips pressed into a thin line. "Your Majesty," she said curtly, rising to her feet.

"Now, now," he said, his voice lilting with mock offense. "No need to be so formal. How many times must I tell you to call me Darius?"

Irene's jaw tightened as I hid a smile. Their interactions were always... entertaining.

"Your Majesty," she repeated pointedly, ignoring his correction, "I have delivered my report to the council. If there's nothing further—"

"Oh, there's always something further," he interrupted, stepping closer. "For instance, why do you insist on avoiding me?"

"I am not avoiding you," Irene said, her voice steady though her cheeks betrayed a faint blush.

The emperor chuckled, clearly enjoying himself. "You're terrible at lying, Irene."

Irene turned to me, her exasperation plain. "Veronica, tell him I am not avoiding him."

I raised my hands in mock surrender. "I'm just an innocent bystander," I said, though the amused glint in my eyes earned a glare from her.

"See?" the emperor said smugly, crossing his arms. "Even the duchess knows you're avoiding me."

Before Irene could respond, Alicia's voice cut through the tension. "Duchess! Dominic's trying to eat my doll!"

I stood quickly, suppressing a laugh as I moved to rescue Alicia's doll from my son's curious grasp. Out of the corner of my eye, I saw Irene use the distraction to gather her robes and make a hasty exit.

"Always running," the emperor muttered, his smirk softening into something more contemplative as he watched her retreating figure.

When I returned to my seat, the emperor was still staring after her, his expression unreadable.

"Trouble in paradise?" I teased lightly.

He blinked, turning his attention back to me. "Paradise, Duchess?" he echoed with a sardonic laugh. "Hardly. That woman is impossible."

"Impossible enough to keep your attention for two years," I pointed out, arching an eyebrow.

He opened his mouth to retort but thought better of it, shaking his head instead. "You're meddling, Veronica."

"Call it an observation," I said with a smile.

Before the conversation could continue, Henrick appeared at the doorway, his presence as commanding as ever. His gaze softened as it landed on me, and he gave a slight nod toward the door.

"Veronica," he said simply, extending his hand.

I rose, slipping my hand into his, and the warmth of his touch sent a familiar comfort through me. "We're heading home?"

He nodded. "The twins need their rest."

As we made our way out of the palace, Dominic nestled against Henrick's broad shoulder while I carried a drowsy Dahlia. Glancing back, I caught a final glimpse of the emperor, now leaning against the balcony rail, his gaze fixed on the garden path where Irene had disappeared.

There was something there—something unspoken between them. A tension, a connection, a story waiting to unfold.

And though I was curious, my thoughts turned back to my own little family. Whatever awaited Ezra and Irene, it wasn't my place to interfere. For now, my focus was on the people who mattered most to me.

The carriage ride back to Audovera Castle was peaceful, save for Dahlia's occasional babbling as she clung to my sleeve. Dominic, ever the quiet one, was already fast asleep in Henrick's arms, his tiny hand gripping the fabric of his father's coat.

Henrick caught me staring and raised a brow. "What is it?"

"Nothing," I said, shaking my head with a soft smile. "It's just... moments like this make everything worthwhile."

He smirked, leaning closer. "You're getting sentimental, Veronica."

"Blame the twins," I teased. "Motherhood has made me soft."

His chuckle was low and warm, and for a moment, the weight of everything else fell away.

When we reached the castle, the maids hurried to greet us, whisking the twins away for their afternoon nap. I lingered in the hall, watching as Henrick exchanged a few words with one of his knights before dismissing him.

"Will you be busy again tonight?" I asked, unable to hide the note of disappointment in my voice.

Henrick turned to me, his expression softening. "No. I'm all yours tonight."

A rush of warmth filled my chest, and I nodded, already looking forward to a quiet evening together.

But as I turned to head toward the nursery, a knock at the door caught my attention. A footman appeared, bowing deeply. "Your Grace, a letter from the palace."

I frowned, taking the sealed parchment. Henrick's brows furrowed as he stepped closer. "What is it?"

"I don't know," I murmured, breaking the seal.

The handwriting was unmistakably Irene's.

Duchess Veronica, I need to speak with you. It's urgent. Please meet me at the temple garden at your earliest convenience.—Irene

I handed the letter to Henrick, who scanned it quickly. His jaw tightened, but he said nothing.

"I'll go," I said softly.

He nodded, though his gaze lingered. "Be careful."

The temple garden was quiet when I arrived, the soft glow of twilight casting long shadows across the stone paths. Irene was waiting near the fountain, her usual composed demeanor replaced by something more restless.

"Irene," I called gently, and she turned, relief washing over her face.

"Thank you for coming," she said, stepping closer.

"What's wrong?" I asked, my concern growing.

She hesitated, her fingers twisting in the fabric of her robe. "It's about the emperor."

I blinked, caught off guard. "The emperor?"

Irene sighed, sinking onto the edge of the fountain. "He's... he's insufferable, Veronica. Always teasing, always prying. And yet—" She broke off, shaking her head.

"And yet?" I prompted, sitting beside her.

Her hands tightened in her lap. "And yet, I can't seem to stay away. Every time I try to keep my distance, he finds a way to pull me back. I don't know what to do."

I studied her, noting the flush in her cheeks and the way her voice wavered. Irene was always calm, always in control. To see her like this... it was startling.

"You care for him," I said softly.

She didn't deny it. Instead, her silence spoke volumes.

"Irene, I've known you long enough to see when something's weighing on you. If you feel something for him, maybe it's worth exploring."

She laughed bitterly. "He's the emperor, Veronica. And I'm just a priestess. Whatever I feel doesn't matter."

"It matters to him," I said gently.

Her head shot up, her eyes searching mine. "What do you mean?"

I hesitated, choosing my words carefully. "I've seen the way he looks at you, Irene. There's something there. He wouldn't tease you so much if you didn't mean anything to him."

Her lips parted as if to argue, but no words came. Finally, she sighed, burying her face in her hands. "This is so complicated."

"Love usually is," I said with a smile.

Her head snapped up, a spark of indignation in her eyes. "Who said anything about love?"

I raised a brow. "Oh, please. If it's not love, then what is it?"

She groaned, burying her face in her hands again, and I couldn't help but laugh.

When I returned to the castle, the conversation lingered in my mind. Henrick was waiting for me in the study, a glass of wine in hand.

"Everything alright?" he asked as I stepped into the room.

I nodded, sinking into the chair across from him. "Irene is... in a bit of a situation."

"With the emperor?"

I blinked, startled. "You knew?"

Henrick smirked. "It's hard not to notice. The emperor's been unusually... distracted these past few days"

I shook my head, amazed at how much Henrick saw without saying. "Do you think it'll work out between them?"

His smirk softened into a thoughtful smile. "If anyone can keep with the emperor in line, it's Irene."

I laughed, the tension of the day finally easing. "You're probably right."

And as we sat there, the warmth of the fire casting a soft glow around us, I couldn't help but feel grateful—for my family, for my friends, and for the quiet moments that made life so beautifully unpredictable.

Chapter 16

The next morning, I found myself walking through the castle gardens with Dominic and Dahlia toddling beside me. Dahlia clutched a bundle of freshly picked daisies in her tiny hands, proudly presenting them to every passing servant, while Dominic focused on chasing butterflies with an unwavering determination.

Henrick watched us from a distance, leaning against one of the stone arches. His gaze was soft, a rare expression that made my heart flutter.

"Are you just going to stand there and admire us all day?" I called out, a teasing lilt in my voice.He straightened, a smirk tugging at his lips. "I'm considering it."

Before I could respond, one of the knights approached, bowing deeply. "Your Grace, there's a message from the palace."

I exchanged a glance with Henrick as he took the letter, his brows knitting together as he read.

"What is it?" I asked, scooping up Dominic as he made a beeline for the fountain.

"The emperor has summoned us for a banquet," Henrick said, his tone neutral.

"A banquet?" I repeated, shifting Dahlia to my other arm as she reached for her brother. "For what occasion?"

"It doesn't say," Henrick replied, folding the letter. "But knowing the emperor, he probably just wants an excuse to show off."

I chuckled, but a flicker of unease settled in my chest. After yesterday's conversation with Irene, I couldn't help but wonder if this had something to do with her.

That evening, we arrived at the palace. The grand hall was already buzzing with activity, nobles clad in their finest gowns and suits mingling beneath glittering chandeliers.

Henrick stayed close to me, his hand resting lightly on my back as we navigated the crowd. Dominic and Dahlia were left in the care of their nannies for the evening, much to their dismay.

"Veronica, you made it!"

I turned to see Irene approaching, her usual priestess attire replaced by an elegant blue gown that brought out the color of her eyes. She looked stunning, but her nervous smile told me she was far from comfortable.

"You look beautiful," I said warmly, taking her hands in mine.

"And you look like you belong on a throne," she replied with a small laugh.

Henrick raised a brow. "Should I be worried?"

"Always," I teased, earning a chuckle from Irene.

Before we could say more, a loud voice boomed across the hall.

"Welcome, everyone!"

The emperor stood at the top of the staircase, his arms spread wide. His golden attire shimmered in the candlelight, and his ever-present smirk was firmly in place.

"Tonight, we celebrate unity, prosperity, and—most importantly—the people who make it all possible." His gaze flickered briefly to Irene, and I didn't miss the way her cheeks flushed.

Henrick leaned down to murmur in my ear. "You were right. He's smitten."

I bit back a smile, watching the emperor descended the staircase. The crowd parted for him, and he made his way directly to Irene.

"Priestess Irene," he said, his voice carrying just enough to be heard by those nearest. "You honor us with your presence."

Irene dipped into a graceful curtsy, though I noticed the slight tremor in her hands. "Your Majesty, the honor is mine."

Their exchange was polite, formal even, but there was an undeniable tension between them."Do you think he'll ever admit it?" I whispered to Henrick.

"That guy? Admit his feelings?" Henrick snorted. "Not unless someone forces it out of him."The rest of the evening passed in a blur of conversation and laughter, but my attention kept drifting back to Irene and the emperor. They were never far from each other, their interactions charged with an energy that was impossible to ignore.

Later that night, as the banquet wound down, I found myself alone with Irene on one of the palace balconies. The cool night air was a welcome relief after the heat of the crowded hall."He's impossible," Irene said suddenly, breaking the silence.

I turned to her with a knowing smile. "Hmm?"

She groaned, leaning against the railing. "One moment, he's teasing me like a child, and the next, he's looking at me like I'm the only person in the room. I don't know how to deal with him.""Maybe you don't have to," I suggested.

She frowned. "What do you mean?"

"Maybe it's not about figuring him out," I said gently. "Maybe it's about letting things unfold naturally. He clearly cares about you, Irene. And from what I've seen, you care about him too."Her expression softened, though doubt lingered in her eyes. "It's not that simple, Veronica. He's the emperor. Our lives are worlds apart."

"Love doesn't care about titles," I said with a shrug.

Irene laughed, though there was a trace of sadness in her voice. "You make it sound so easy."

"It's not," I admitted. "But if anyone can navigate this, it's you. You're stronger than you think, Irene."

She gave me a small, grateful smile. "Thank you."

When Henrick and I returned to Audovera Castle that night, I couldn't shake the feeling that something significant had shifted. Irene and the emperor's story was far from over, and I couldn't wait to see how it unfolded.

As I settled into bed beside Henrick, his arm draped protectively around me, I whispered, "Do you think they'll find their way?"

"They will," he murmured, his voice thick with sleep. "If they're anything like us, they will."

The moon cast its silver glow over the quiet halls of Audovera Castle as I found myself sitting by the window in the nursery. Dominic and Dahlia were fast asleep, their rhythmic breathing filling the room with a sense of peace. A book lay forgotten in my lap as my thoughts drifted far away—to a time when Adelaide, the late Empress, still graced this world with her quiet strength and kindness.

I ran a hand through Dahlia's soft curls, and for a moment, I imagined Adelaide's gentle smile watching over us.

"Adelaide," I whispered, my voice barely audible over the crackling of the nearby fire.

She had been more than an empress; she was a friend, a sister in spirit. From the moment we met, I admired her grace and the steadfast love she had for her family, especially for her daughter, Princess Alicia.

I remembered the long afternoons in the palace gardens, where she and I would sit on the marble benches, watching Alicia chase butterflies or collect flowers.

"Veronica," she had said once, her tone contemplative. "Do you think Alicia will remember me if I... if I'm no longer here?"

"Don't say things like that," I had scolded her gently, though my heart tightened at the shadow in her eyes.

"I must," she insisted, her fingers brushing a lavender sprig in her hand. "The role of an empress often comes with sacrifices. My health... my time... even my life might not always be mine to keep. But Alicia—she deserves to remember a mother who loves her, not just a queen who ruled."

"She will remember," I had promised her fiercely. "Through me, through everyone who loves you. We'll make sure she knows who you were."

Adelaide had smiled at that, a bittersweet curve of her lips. "You're her aunt in all but name, Veronica. If the day comes that I can no longer guide her, I hope you'll be there."

A sharp ache filled my chest as the memory faded. I blinked away the tears that threatened to fall, looking down at Dominic and Dahlia. I had kept that promise. I visited Princess Alicia often, sharing stories about her mother, ensuring that the little girl never felt alone.

But now, things were changing.

Irene.

Adelaide would have adored her. I was sure of it.

The thought brought a small smile to my face. Irene wasn't like the other women at court. She wasn't driven by ambition or blinded by power. Her strength came from her faith, her compassion, and her unwavering dedication to others.

Adelaide would have seen that. She would have known that Irene was the kind of woman the emperor needed—not as a queen for the empire, but as a partner for the man beneath the crown.

Adelaide once confided in me about her fears for the emperor.

"He carries the weight of the empire on his shoulders," she had said, her voice laced with worry. "He needs someone who can lighten that burden, someone who can remind him that he's human."

At the time, I thought she had meant herself. Now, I realized she had been speaking of someone like Irene.

I could almost hear Adelaide's laughter in my mind. "Of course it would be Irene," she would say with a playful twinkle in her eye. "Who else could handle someone as infuriating as Darius?"

I laughed softly to myself, earning a sleepy murmur from Dominic. I smoothed his hair and kissed his forehead.

"I promise, Adelaide," I whispered into the quiet of the room. "I'll make sure your daughter is safe and loved. And if Irene is meant to stand beside Darius, I'll support her as you would have."

Chapter 17

The next day, as I stood in the gardens of the palace with Alicia by my side, I felt a sense of calm wash over me. Irene approached us with her usual warm smile, a bouquet of fresh flowers in her hands.

"Duchess Veronica," Alicia said, tugging on my sleeve. "Do you think Mama would like these flowers?"

I crouched down to meet her gaze, brushing a strand of hair from her face. "She'd love them, sweetheart. Just like she loves you."

Irene knelt beside Alicia, her expression tender. "Why don't we plant them together in her memory?"

Alicia's eyes lit up, and she nodded enthusiastically.

As we worked together in the soil, I caught Irene glancing toward the palace, her gaze lingering on the balcony where the emperor stood watching us.

Adelaide, I thought, wherever you are, I hope you're smiling. Because in Irene, I see a future where your daughter will grow up surrounded by love and guidance. And the emperor... he'll find the balance he's been searching for.

For the first time in a long while, I felt a sense of closure. Adelaide's legacy was in safe hands—and so was the empire.

The next morning, I found myself walking along the cobblestone paths of the imperial gardens, with Alicia skipping beside me. Her laughter filled the crisp air as she clutched a bundle of flowers Irene had helped her pick earlier.

"Slow down, Alicia," I called, though my voice held no urgency. Watching her carefree smile reminded me of how much she had grown in these past two years. The memory of Adelaide lingered in her features—her delicate nose, her soulful eyes—but Alicia's spirit was undeniably her own.

Irene walked a few paces behind us, her serene presence as comforting as the morning sun. Despite her priestly robes, there was an elegance to her steps, a quiet strength that made her seem as though she belonged in the imperial gardens as much as any empress.

"Are you sure I should be here, Veronica?" Irene asked after a while, her voice low but tinged with concern.

I turned back to her, arching a brow. "And why not? Alicia adores you, and so does everyone else who matters."

She hesitated, her hands clasped together. "The court doesn't see it that way. Many still think I'm unfit to be here, let alone... to stand beside the emperor."

Irene rarely spoke of the whispers that followed her through the palace halls, but I knew they existed. Nobles with too much time on their hands and too little faith in the emperor's choices.

"You're stronger than their words," I said firmly. "And besides, do you really think the emperor cares what they think? The man has been teasing you mercilessly for two years. If he had any doubt about you, he'd have found someone else to torment by now."

Irene let out a soft laugh, though her cheeks turned pink. "He does have a talent for being infuriating."

"That's putting it mildly."

We both chuckled, and Alicia glanced back at us, confused.

"What's funny?" she asked, her head tilting.

"Just grown-up talk," I said, ruffling her hair.

Alicia wrinkled her nose. "Grown-ups are boring."

Irene knelt beside her, placing a gentle hand on her shoulder. "Not all grown-ups, little one. Some of us are quite fun, don't you think?"

Alicia giggled and nodded, pointing at me. "Duchess Veronica's fun!"

"And what about me?" Irene asked, her tone playful.

Alicia paused, tapping her chin dramatically before breaking into a grin. "You're fun, too!"

The warmth in Irene's eyes was undeniable as she pulled Alicia into a brief hug. It was a small moment, but it spoke volumes.

As we continued walking, we eventually reached a quiet corner of the gardens where Adelaide's favorite flowers—lavenders and white roses—bloomed in abundance. It was a space I had visited often with Alicia, a sanctuary where we could feel Adelaide's presence.

Alicia ran ahead, her small hands brushing the flowers as she hummed a tune I recognized as one Adelaide used to sing. I stood beside Irene, watching her with a mix of pride and melancholy.

"There you are."

Both Irene and I turned to see the emperor approaching, his usual confident stride tempered by a rare softness in his expression. His gaze flickered to Alicia first, ensuring she was safe, before settling on Irene.

"Busy day, Your Majesty?" I teased, trying to lighten the sudden tension that always seemed to hang in the air when the two of them were together.

The emperor smirked. "Busier now that I've found my wayward priestess wandering the gardens again."

Irene rolled her eyes but said nothing, her cheeks flushing ever so slightly.

"Come, Alicia," I called, breaking the moment. "Let's leave the emperor and his priestess to their business."

Alicia pouted but obeyed, skipping back to my side as I began leading her toward the castle.

"Veronica," Irene said suddenly, her voice stopping me in my tracks.

I turned to look at her.

"Thank you," she said simply, her expression sincere.

I nodded, understanding the depth of her gratitude without needing further explanation.

As Alicia and I walked away, I glanced back one last time. The emperor and Irene stood close, their conversation too quiet for me to hear.

Adelaide, I thought with a bittersweet smile, you were right. Irene is exactly who he needs. And I'll make sure she finds her place, just as you would have wanted.

The future of the empire felt brighter than ever.

Epilogue

Time had passed since that pivotal day when the future of the empire had been set in motion. The world around us had changed, but what remained constant was the bond between the emperor and Irene, who had now fully embraced her role as empress. Their love, once hesitant and clouded by uncertainty, had blossomed into something undeniably strong—something that not only united them but also united the empire.

It was a beautiful morning when the emperor and Irene stood together at the heart of the palace gardens, hand in hand, as they greeted their subjects. The garden had been meticulously maintained, flowers in full bloom, and birds chirping their morning songs. It was a day for celebration—a day to mark the new chapter in their lives, as a couple and as rulers.

I watched from a distance, a smile curling on my lips as I cradled Dominic in my arms and held Dahlia's hand. Henrick stood beside me, his arm around my waist, his warmth anchoring me in this moment of joy.

It was incredible to think about how far we had come. From the uncertainty and pain of the past to this moment—where the emperor and Irene were finally at peace, not just with each other, but with themselves.

Emperor Darius and Irene had found a rhythm in their relationship, one built on trust and shared responsibility. Their love had been tested through time, through the battles they had faced—both external and internal—but it had emerged stronger, unshakable. It was not just a partnership of power; it was a partnership of hearts.

As I watched them interact, it was clear that Irene was no longer the quiet, reserved priestess who had once been unsure of her place in the world. She had become a fierce and compassionate empress, someone who would stand beside Darius, not as a mere support, but as an equal, a partner in every sense of the word.

The day was filled with laughter and joy. A feast was held in honor of the newly strengthened empire, and the palace was filled with guests—nobles, friends, and families from every corner of the land. The sounds of celebration echoed through the halls, a stark contrast to the silence of those earlier years.

At the heart of the celebration was Irene and Darius, the emperor and his empress, standing together in the center of the ballroom. Their smiles were radiant, their hands clasped tightly, the weight of the empire now shared between them. Irene had never looked more beautiful, her grace and strength evident in every step she took. And Darius—proud and content—looked at her with the kind of adoration that only true love could bring.

They were ready. Ready to rule, ready to lead, and ready to love each other for all the days to come.

Later that evening, as the festivities began to wind down and the stars began to twinkle above, I found myself in the quiet of the palace garden once again. Henrick was beside me, and our children, Dominic and Dahlia, had fallen asleep in the nursery. It was a rare moment of peace, and I cherished it.

The soft rustling of leaves in the breeze was the only sound that filled the space. I leaned against Henrick, letting the cool night air wash over me.

"I'm proud of you, Veronica," Henrick said quietly, his voice filled with warmth.

I looked up at him, my heart swelling with love. "We've all come so far, haven't we?"

He nodded, a soft smile on his lips. "Yes, we have. And it's not just about the empire or the crown. It's about us—about our family. I couldn't ask for more."

His words wrapped around me like a warm embrace, and I knew that, no matter what challenges lay ahead, we would face them together.

Twenty years had passed since the dawn of the new era. The once-bustling halls of the Audovera castle were now filled with a sense of history and legacy. The empire had grown stronger, and the Audovera family had firmly established themselves at the heart of it all. The twins, Dominic and Dahlia, now stood as young adults, their paths stretching ahead of them, ready to take on the mantle of leadership in their own unique ways.

Dominic Audovera, with his striking dark hair and sharp, commanding presence, had grown into a young man of exceptional strength and intellect. His father, Duke Henrick, had often said that Dominic would be a natural leader, and the people of Audovera had already begun to recognize him for his unwavering resolve and commitment to the duchy. Though still learning the intricacies of governance, Dominic's wisdom and keen sense of justice were apparent to all who knew him.

But there was more to Dominic than just his public image. Behind the stern demeanor, he had inherited his mother's warmth—though he showed it in quieter, more subtle ways. It was often said that when Dominic spoke, people listened. He carried himself with the confidence and grace that only years of careful guidance from both his parents could provide.

He stood now, watching over the grand courtyard of the Audovera estate, his gaze sharp as he surveyed the training grounds. The knights were hard at work, and he took a quiet satisfaction in knowing that the future of Audovera was in capable hands, whether it was in battle or diplomacy. His mother's legacy, and his own determination, would guide them forward.

Dahlia Audovera, on the other hand, was a vision of elegance and wisdom that surpassed her years. Tall, poised, and with the same silver-gray eyes as her mother, Dahlia had inherited the strategic mind of her father, the Duke. Her sharp intellect was coupled with an innate ability to connect with others, making her a formidable presence at the palace and in political circles.

She had always stood by Dominic's side, offering her insight when needed, though her talents were often seen as more subtle. Where Dominic was direct, Dahlia knew when to weave words carefully, using her diplomacy to bring opposing sides together. It was no surprise that the emperor had come to rely on her as an advisor, often seeking her counsel on matters of state.

Now, as a young woman of noble standing, Dahlia was beginning to take on more public roles. She attended political functions, often by her father's side, representing the Audovera family with poise. She had learned the value of family and loyalty, always placing her loved ones at the center of her heart, and she had an unwavering dedication to her people.

One evening, as the sun dipped below the horizon, casting a golden hue across the palace gardens, the family gathered on the balcony to celebrate the twins' coming of age. The occasion was not only a celebration of their growth but also a reminder of the legacy that they would continue to carry.

Henrick and Veronica stood together, their hands intertwined, as they watched Dominic and Dahlia interact with the guests. A quiet pride settled over them, knowing that their children had flourished beyond their expectations.

"It feels like just yesterday we were holding them in our arms," Veronica said softly, a nostalgic smile playing on her lips.

Henrick chuckled, his eyes crinkling with the warmth of shared memories. "Time flies. But they've grown into fine young adults. I'm proud of them."

Veronica's heart swelled with love as she watched Dominic and Dahlia laugh with their friends. "I never imagined how much joy they would bring us. And now, they're going to lead the way for the next generation."

Henrick's gaze shifted to the twins, his expression thoughtful. "They'll do more than that. They'll redefine what it means to be a leader, just like you did, Veronica."

The next day, the twins stood before the people of Audovera, ready to make their first major address to the public as the future leaders of the duchy. The ceremony was symbolic, as the family passed on the torch to the next generation. Their parents, standing by their side, couldn't help but feel a bittersweet pride in knowing that their children were now the ones carrying the legacy forward.

Dominic stepped up first, his voice steady and firm as he addressed the crowd. "As we stand here today, it is with honor that I accept the responsibility that comes with my title. I will work tirelessly to protect our lands, our people, and the values that have made Audovera strong. Together, with my sister, we will lead this duchy into a new era."

Dahlia followed, her voice a soft contrast to her brother's, yet equally powerful. "We will ensure that the future is one of peace and prosperity. And we will do so with the wisdom and guidance our parents have shown us. We are ready to take on the challenges ahead, as a family and as the people of Audovera."

The crowd erupted into applause, their cheers echoing throughout the courtyard. It was a moment of triumph, but also of reflection. The future was bright, and the Audovera family was ready to step into the next chapter with confidence, love, and unwavering dedication.

As the sun set on that monumental day, Veronica and Henrick stood together, watching as their children took their place as the new leaders of the duchy. The legacy they had built was now in the hands of Dominic and Dahlia, and they couldn't have been prouder.

"Look at them," Henrick said softly, his arm around Veronica's shoulders. "They've made us proud, haven't they?"

Veronica nodded, her heart full. "Yes. They've created a future that's even brighter than we could have imagined."

And so, the Audovera family continued on, with Dominic and Dahlia at the helm, leading with wisdom, compassion, and strength. The empire, and their legacy, would thrive for generations to come.

The story of the Audovera family was far from over—it was just beginning.

www.ingramcontent.com/pod-product-compliance
Lightning Source LLC
Chambersburg PA
CBHW071829190726
48292CB00005B/1683